BEING

WITH

HENRY

A MELANIE KROUPA BOOK

BEING

WITH

HENRY

Martha Brooks

DORLING KINDERSLEY PUBLISHING, INC.

Acknowledgments

The author would like to thank the Manitoba Arts Council and the Canada Council for their continued and deeply appreciated financial support, the wonderful editorial team of Melanie Kroupa at DK Ink and Shelley Tanaka at Groundwood Books, and, as well, Maureen Hunter and Alice Drader for generous readings and advice.

Two sections of *Being with Henry* appeared in slightly different form as part of the story "The Kindness of Strangers," from the collection *Traveling on into the Light and Other Stories.* The author is grateful to Orchard Books, New York, and to Groundwood Books, Toronto, for permission to quote, in this manner, her own work.

A Melanie Kroupa Book

Dorling Kindersley Publishing, Inc., 95 Madison Avenue, New York, New York 10016
Visit us on the World Wide Web at http://www.dk.com

Dorling Kindersley books are available at special discounts for bulk purchases for sales promotions or premiums. Special editions, including personalized covers, excerpts of existing guides, and corporate imprints can be created in large quantities for specific needs. For more information, contact Special Markets Dept., Dorling Kindersley Publishing, Inc., 95 Madison Ave., New York, NY 10016; fax: (800) 600-9098.

Library of Congress Cataloging-in-Publication Data
Brooks, Martha [date]
Being with Henry / Martha Brooks
p. cm.
Summary: Forced out of his home by a disagreeable and bullying stepfather, sixteen-year-old Laker moves to another town and strikes up an unexpected friendship with a frail but determined old man.
ISBN: 0-7894-2588-2
[1. Old age—Fiction. 2. Stepfathers—Fiction.] I. Title.
PZ7.B7975 Be 2000
[Fic]—dc21   99-046464

Book design by Jennifer Browne
The text of this book is set in 13 point Baskerville. Printed and bound in the U.S.A.
First Edition, 2000
2 4 6 8 10 9 7 5 3 1

For Vincent Champagne

and for

Gwendoline May Brooks

Sometimes I go about pitying myself,
and all the time
I am being carried on great winds across the sky.
—Anonymous, Chippewa

(adapted by Robert Bly from Frances Densmore's translation)

Our life is a faint tracing on the surface of mystery.
—Annie Dillard

Pilgrim at Tinker Creek

ONE

Dreams and Lies

Journal Entry: In my dream the lake is golden—as if a skin of light is floating on its surface. There's a face beside mine as we bob around in the water—somebody I don't recognize. She's an old woman and she's very brown and her arms hold me, then raise me up. I'm real young, maybe one or two, and she calls me her Sunny Laker Boy. Laker, she says. That's what she names me: Laker. Audrey told me once that I wouldn't remember anything like that. How could I, because it's just a dream, she said, and besides, babies don't remember things.

Audrey showed him a picture of his birth father once. It was taken at a party. His father wore a faded denim shirt and a white shell necklace. He was lean and dark, with a weird, spacey smile, and blond Audrey, on his knee, wore this long, thin, pink dress with a trashy slit that reached well beyond her thigh. Somebody had taken a black marker and drawn a balloon over his father's head, like he was a cartoon character, and inside the balloon were these words: Hey, buddy! Where's my beer?

4   Not exactly any kid's dream photo of Mom and Dad.

He is nine years old when Audrey shows him this photograph. It is a Sunday afternoon. Stepfather number one, whom he hasn't seen since he was five years old, has decided to look them up.

In a very new suit, Reg sits on their very old sofa, and a spring in it comes loose and gives him a boost. Laker laughs and Audrey laughs. Reg leaves.

"I guess it embarrassed him," says Audrey, with a little twisted smile. "He couldn't stand seeing the way we live."

Laker makes her coffee. Puts three sugars into it, taking care to stir it twelve times so that everything is dissolved and very sweet.

She sits on the floor in front of the sofa, beside a pile of books they selected together, the previous day, at the library. A cigarette grows a long, pale ash in the ashtray. Her long, thin, stick legs make a V in front of her, and between them is the red and green Christmas-colored sewing box where she also puts personal papers. She keeps wiping away big tears and is trying to find something. He sits down, sets her coffee beside her, strokes her back with one hand. He hates his stupid stepfather for coming around and making her cry. Finally she takes out an old Polaroid photograph, which she hands to him.

"Laker," she says, *"that's* your father." She pulls him against her chest, where he can hear her beating heart. "That's your *real* father. Did I ever tell you how you got your name?"

He shakes his head, nestles closer.

"Laker," she says again, this time with her little-girl giggle, "you were conceived during an L.A. Lakers game. And he . . . your real dad . . . he really liked basketball." She kisses the top of his head, hugging him against her so hard he misses a breath.

This is a confusing moment. Later, he goes into the bathroom and looks at his own face in the mirror. Except for his dark hair and dark eyes, all he sees is a male version of blond Audrey. It's as if almost nothing from his birth father's gene pool has been offered up. As if he's been cut out of his mother's side, so that the two of them float weightless and unbelonging in this world.

There were mornings when Audrey didn't get out of bed. Handing him a crumpled piece of paper with the phone number of her latest employer, she'd say, "Call them for me, will you, honey?"

"I don't know what to tell them, Audrey."

"Well, Laker, honey, make up some excuse. Okay? Will you do that for me? I just can't do this today."

So there he was, this kid, making the call. But he had soon discovered that he could put on a voice—

like an older brother or a husband. Amazingly, whenever he needed it, it was simply there. It was all in the way he told the lie, his voice sincere and deep: "Her mother is dying of a brain tumor. And the family is very close. Naturally, she needs time to be with her." The person on the other end of the line, who only seconds before was ready to give Audrey Wyatt the sack, suddenly turned soft and serious. What kind of bastard would fire a woman whose mother was dying of a brain tumor?

A few days later Audrey would go back, work sporadically for a couple more weeks, and then they'd fire her. At the time, they were living in Minneapolis, had been evicted from three different places, but they stayed in the same neighborhood. He went to the same school, eventually got some baby-sitting jobs.

Then, a couple of years before stepfather number two, Rick the Prick, came along, he found Mr. and Mrs. Downes. They paid him way over the recommended rate for baby-sitting their little boy, Petey. He never dared to say out loud how much they paid, for fear of somehow jinxing it.

Mr. Downes owned a pizza take-out and delivery, and so there was usually all the pizza and root beer he and Audrey could handle. Then there were these father-to-son talks, about what Mr. Downes called "the mysterious workings of the universe." One eye kind of crossed, and he walked with a limp. He had lost his left leg to cancer. His favorite saying was "Trust the imponderables and things will work out." He'd slap his leg, the artificial one. "After this happened I found Gretel. And that's magic, Laker. That's how the world works if you pay attention."

Mrs. Downes, the beloved Gretel, a former actress, had lived in New York and at one time worked as a body double in a movie starring Robert Duvall. She said he was a very spiritual person. She glowed when she said this. She was a cool lady. She talked to their four-year-old, Petey, like he was the most brilliant child who had ever walked the face of the planet. She bought him books and toys and filled his life with color.

Every summer morning, at about five o'clock, he and Petey and Gretel got into the big, shiny van that Mr. Downes had bought for her, and then they drove about an hour north of Minneapolis, where he looked after Petey while she took up her duties as acting director at a little outdoor theater that put on plays for tourists.

He did this for two summers. To pass the time he acted out stories for Petey, kind of a storybook theater idea. Petey had his favorites: "Do the one with the wolf and the grandmother, okay, Laker?" Or the time he put on full clown makeup and had Petey believing he'd handed him the string of a dragon kite. "I can see it!" said Petey, watching the imaginary blue-and-red silk dragon float miles up into the sky. "Can you see it, too? Can you see it, Laker?"

"Of course." For that moment he really could see it, and he felt proud, like he'd invented something outside the world, something beautiful and perfect and untouchable.

"I like the part about it being a dragon," said Petey. "But it isn't scary, is it?"

"Do you want it to be?"

"Yeah."

Laker laughed. "Okay, it's scary."

Another time he bought Petey a whistle. Just a cheap little wooden thing; two red feathers hung from it, and it made a great piercing sound. The whistle became one of Petey's biggest treasures, which really knocked Laker out. Petey had a little green cotton pullover with a pouch on the front, and most of the time that's where he kept the whistle. He said it had to be kept there because of the feathers. "They might get broken," he told Laker solemnly.

One day Gretel told Petey, "You've worn that top five days in a row. It's got jam all over it. It has to be washed, pumpkin. Here, put on your jacket. It's got lots of pockets. See? Look at all these pockets."

So Petey reluctantly put on the jacket; but on the
way out to Caravan Farm he started crying incon-
solably, leaning against Laker's side.

"Are you worried?" asked Laker.

Petey nodded his head.

"When we get there we'll go to the costume de-
partment," said Laker. "We'll find a piece of leather
and make something for it, okay?"

"What kind of thing?"

"Like a pouch. On a string. You could wear it
around your neck. The feathers would be protected.
You'd never lose it."

Petey rubbed his eyes. "I want a red pouch."

"I'll see what I can do."

"It *has* to be red. *Promise* me."

"Okay. I promise. It'll be red."

It was amazing what they found—a piece of soft,
rusty red suede. Material for the pouch, a little
fringe, and a drawstring big enough to slip over
Petey's head.

"See?" Petey skipped over to Gretel, who crouched
so he could proudly show her the pouch hanging
from his neck.

"That's so imaginative," said Gretel. "What a great
idea."

"He's my best friend," Petey told her.

"I can see that," she said, smiling up at Laker.

It was a moment that filled him with light. For a long time after that, he would examine this little piece of time in his mind, slowing it down, stretching it out, especially the part where Gretel told him he was imaginative. The intriguing way she had said this, as if imagination was what they all had in common, seemed to mark him as belonging to them, and that felt terrific.

In the mornings he and Petey always played flat out, and then Petey had his snack. After that he'd have one of his kid sleeps, which also knocked Laker out—the way little kids could drop in their tracks, anywhere, and be dead to the world within moments. Laker cuddled him against his side and, for the next hour or so, watched the actors rehearse on the little stage under the green trees, or sometimes he read. Over those two summers, he must have read at least fifty plays—all stuff Gretel loaned him. "To fuel your mind," she said, handing him Tennessee Williams's *A Streetcar Named Desire,* which became his favorite play of all. He loved the final scene where the frail and crazy Blanche DuBois says, "Whoever you are—I have always depended on the kindness of strangers."

Gretel told him, "When you're an actor you take all the things that have happened to you and turn them into art." For a while he even thought about becoming an actor. It seemed a sensible way to try and figure things out. And it would have been great to belong to what Gretel called the "theater family."

Audrey had actually held a job since the beginning of May. She seemed pretty happy. She worked for Gretel, sewing costumes and sometimes acting as prop mistress and whatever else needed doing at the Caravan Farm Theater Company.

But then, in early August of that second summer, Audrey meets some trucker outside the Safeway store two blocks down the street from their apartment. He's hauling a load of frozen fish and pulls into the parking lot just as skinny Audrey is flying along like Olive Oyl in that old Popeye movie, wearing big brown boots and bright pink tights and the strange floaty tunic she made herself from a picture she saw in *Vogue* magazine.

He imagines it all as she stands in their apartment waving her arms and recounting it—the quite specific cartoon quality of the scene. They're both laughing. Right up until the part where the guy rams on his brakes, gets down out of his rig, and starts screaming obscenities at her like some half-crazed maniac.

"I guess I really scared him," she says, looking around the living room of their cramped apartment with that lost-little-girl look she sometimes gets.

He's been trying to cruise the channels, but the batteries on their TV remote are running low. "Guy sounds like a prick. You have to be careful of guys like that, Audrey."

"Oh, stop being so protective. It'll be fine." She gives him a sudden smile like the sun just came out. "Besides, you're going to be meeting him. Very soon. So be nice."

"I'll be *meeting* him? You're joking, right?"

"His name is Rick. After he calmed down we got talking. And he was all apologetic. He's been on a long haul all the way from the coast. Owns his own truck. Can you believe it? Those rigs cost a fortune." She's eating a poverty sandwich—bread, catsup, a little sliced onion. She puts down the sandwich, licks her fingers, runs off to the bathroom, and starts up the shower.

Rick arrives at the door an hour later. Skinny, short, wiry, with a prominent jaw and a way of never looking you in the eye. Like the dog that showed up at Caravan Farm early that summer and then never left, always sneaking up behind you, lurching in to take a nip at the backs of your legs.

Next thing, within two and a half months of their

first calamitous meeting, Audrey and Rick are getting married. "Rick is a good man, honey," she says.
"You'll get used to him. He just has a different way
about him."

"Are you crazy? Think about it. He doesn't even
have a sense of humor. And he's an asshole."

"Now watch your language," she says primly.

"Since *when?* My God, this is a totally warped bad
dream. Mom, don't do this, okay? Why do you have
to marry him?"

"Laker, he works hard and he wants to take care of
us. Why is this so bad?"

"Because *I* can take care of you," he says despcr-
ately. "Let me do that, okay? I can get another job. A
real job. I can take care of us both. Let me do that.
Please?"

"Laker," says Audrey, with a sad little twist of her
mouth, "you're just a kid."

Gretel and Mr. Downes host an outdoor wedding
in their huge back yard. Many of the people from
Caravan Farm Theater Company attend. The bride's
tamed hair is combed back and fastened with a silver
clip for the occasion. Rick has chosen her dress. It's
form-fitting, short and white, with a tiny jacket tossed
over her thin shoulders.

The Downeses have hired Laker's replacement,
because tomorrow he'll be leaving with Audrey and

Rick, moving to Duluth. The girl, whose name is Rachel, has pale eyes, and for most of the afternoon obligingly carries Petey upside down. "It's his new thing," Laker explains to her. "He's been in his upside-down mode for almost three weeks now."

Petey slides off her neck, does a somersault, jumps up and throws himself around Laker's legs. "Tomorrow," he says, looking up at Laker, "will you play clown with me?"

"Can't, sport," says Laker, ruffling Petey's silky hair. Then he leaves his hand there. Petey's face is flushed. He smells like grass and ice cream. Laker can't stand how sad all of this is making him feel.

"Then what will we play?"

"We can play anything you like," says Rachel, quickly.

"But Laker will play with us," says Petey, with downcast eyes.

"I told you, remember? I have to go away."

"When you come back we'll play clown, okay, Laker?"

The wedding reception goes on for hours, with tables of food, lined-up liquor bottles, dancing and singing on the lawn. Laker sinks into the shadows and tosses back a few two-ounce shots of Johnnie Walker from the bottle he lifted when the bartender Mr. Downes hired for the event took a bathroom

break. After his tongue begins to feel numb, he finally stumbles out of the gazebo where he's been sitting, slumped and unnoticed, because everyone else
is having such a whale of a time. He weaves across
the garden. He stands for a while eyeing the goldfish
in the pond that Mr. Downes coaxes back to its former glory every spring. Then there is a break in his
memory until he collapses on the lawn, face down in
his own puke.

Gretel Downes is sitting on the edge of the bed in
her pale yellow guest room. He's lying under an orange quilt, wearing only his underwear. The pair
that has a fairly large hole in the left cheek.
Embarrassment sweeps along his body. Gretel is a
lushly round, incredible woman. She has shiny, wavy
black hair. The face of an angel. Now here she is,
frowning at him. Did he just strip down in front of
everybody in the garden? Before he passed out?

"You poisoned yourself," says Gretel, with an unwa-
vering, worried gaze. He realizes that she is also a little drunk, and finds this oddly comforting. She
places a cool hand on his forehead, firmly pats it,
and pronounces, "But you'll be okay. Sleep it off,
kid."

She gets up, weaving slightly as she crosses the
room, turns out the light, and leaves him alone with

16   a clock that doesn't work and is stuck at one-forty-seven.

Next morning Audrey and Rick come to pick him up. Rick has packed up his semitrailer with all their things.

"How're you doing, hotshot?" Rick claps him on the back. "You really tied one on." There is an edge of pride in his voice.

"You all right, honey?" Audrey, reaching out, pushes back Laker's hair. He shakes her hand away.

"Come on, let's go," says Rick. "We haven't got all day. Let me help you up there, little lady." He opens the cab door and pats Audrey's ass several times.

Laker quickly turns back to the Downeses. Suddenly realizes this is it. He's really leaving them. He raises his hand in a little wave.

Petey, standing beside his parents, looks grave and bewildered. Suddenly he comes running toward Laker, who bends down, expecting a hug.

Petey stops short of the hug, though. He just looks at Laker as if he's finally figured something out. He says, "How will you know what I look like when you're far away?"

"I don't know. I guess I'll have to imagine it." Laker pauses, then adds, "Like at the theater."

Petey pulls off the pouch that hangs around his neck. He tries to fit the drawstring over Laker's head.

It's too small. Now Petey is crying. Laker struggles to find his voice. It's only because Petey really needs him to that he finally manages: "You're sure you want to give this to me?"

Petey nods. Pushes the pouch into Laker's hand.

"I'll take care of it, then. Can I have my hug now?"

Petey tearfully shakes his head and backs away and then comes rushing into his arms, hugging Laker so fiercely that he thinks his heart will break.

Journal Entry: I am in her arms, clinging to her. We are in the lake. She carries me toward the shore. "Look, Laker Boy," she says. With one finger she lifts a huge turquoise dragonfly out of the water. It clings to her, too, until it becomes braver and staggers up her wet brown arm, shivering its wings the whole time. Then up it flies. We watch it dart and dance over the trees into the hills. "Did you like that, my baby?" she asks me. I tell her yes I like that and hug her tight. Her neck is soft and crinkly and smells of the lake and sunlight and the warm sweet wind.

2

Family scene, New Year's Eve. He's getting ready to go out. Rick, in a suit, is smoking a cigarette in the living room. Audrey's in the bathroom fixing herself up.

She's wearing a lurid purple dress that Rick bought her, humming a little song, dabbing perfume between her breasts. "Well, don't you look handsome," she says, glancing at Laker in the mirror. She turns and lightly adjusts the collar on his shirt.

"I need a few bucks, Mom."

Audrey smiles at being called Mom, and says softly, "I'll go ask Rick."

"No. Don't do that. Don't you have any?"

"He gave me grocery money. Maybe I could spare a twenty."

"That'd be great," says Laker, relieved.

"He says you need to find a job." Audrey frowns, waits expectantly.

"I'll start looking next week."

"That's what you said before Christmas."

"I don't want to be a baby-sitter again."

"Rick says that you're shirking your responsibilities."

"Rick can blow it out his ear. It's none of his business what I do."

"He pays all the bills." Audrey turns to the mirror to apply a second coat of mascara. "You could act a little more grateful."

The party he's been invited to is stupid. Somebody drove a Ford Cherokee onto Emily Horton's front lawn and hung it up on a snowbank. A bunch of people are trying to push it out and the guy driving, his head hanging out the window, is totally wasted. The tires spin in ruts that have deepened right down to frozen ground and send off blackened fumes of burning rubber. Laker discovers Emily herself by the fireplace in the family room, sitting on some guy's knee, surrounded by empty beer bottles. The guy has his hand down her pants and she's moaning. Laker leaves, with his own case of beer, goes home, and discovers he has forgotten his house keys. He finds a couple of old blankets in the garage, sits down on Rick's front steps, wraps himself up, cracks open a beer, and drinks a toast to the cold stars.

"What the hell did you think you were doing?" says Rick a couple of hours later. "You could have frozen to death, you stupid kid."

"I forgot my keys."

"Well, that was a genius move."

"Did you have a nice time?" Audrey interjects nervously.

Rick raves on, "Jesus, Audrey, didn't you ever teach your kid nothing? He thinks it's goddamn Florida or something."

"Don't talk to her like that," says Laker.

"I beg your pardon?" says Rick. "Just who do you think you're talking to, buster?"

"You, you half-baked toad."

"*Toad?*" Rick puffs himself up. "I don't need some smart-ass kid calling me a toad."

"Come on," says Audrey. "You're drunk, Rick. Let's go to bed. It's late. It's really late, Rick. Okay? Let's go." She pulls at his sleeve. The veins at the sides of his forehead stand out all ropy and blue in the moonlight.

He doesn't move until after they go in. Then he goes in, himself, and falls onto his bed. He can hear them down the hall, Rick yelling around and Audrey using this pleading, whiny tone that is becoming such a charming part of her personality. To hell with them. The hell with everybody, he thinks, just before he drifts off to sleep.

January is a blur. So are February and March. He can't concentrate on school, doesn't want to hang out with anybody, keeps to himself. He goes to the library, stays like a ghost until closing. He reads a lot of books. The librarians get to know his reading tastes. Plays, plays, and more plays; most specifically any play written by Tennessee Williams.

Sometimes, on their breaks, the librarians sit and talk to him. Most are women. One, whose name is Rebecca, has a great smile. "You're a strange one," she says to him one evening at the end of April. "Don't you have someplace to go?"

He smiles back and shrugs. "I just like coming here."

Rebecca angles her head, piercing him with a look that unveils his heart, and says, "You should apply here. At the library."

"Apply?"

"Look, you seem to be at loose ends," she says delicately. "But you have an obvious passion for books. These days that's kind of a rare thing." She pauses, can see that he is holding his breath, and continues firmly, "There's a library page position opening up. It's minimum wage. Good hours. No guarantees, of course. You might not get hired. But you really should try." She nods several times. He feels an unexpected elation, as if a door has just swung open.

Within ten days, to his astonishment, he has a job at the library. This was probably helped along by the letter of reference that Gretel Downes tucked into his pocket the day they left Minneapolis.

From ex-baby-sitter to library page. He tells Audrey, and she looks relieved. At supper she informs Rick.

"I'll be shelving books. You know, alphabetizing them," Laker explains, "putting them in the right section. Or taking them down and placing them on the order cart. Maybe later I'll get to work at the information desk."

"That should suit you, I guess," says Rick. "At least you'll be pulling in an honest wage. Nothing wrong with that." He actually smiles. Or what passes for a smile—his mouth flattens out until a couple of his teeth show.

Then Rick does the most unexpected thing. He

reaches into his back pocket, pulls out his wallet, and
hands Laker fifty bucks.

"What's this?"

"Use it for anything you like."

"Yeah, but why are you giving it to me?"

Rick bends his head wordlessly over his fish and fries. His hand, the one holding his fork, rests with a slight tremor by his plate. "Audrey," he finally mutters, "you used too goddamn much salt again. And I'd like some ketchup."

Things go along a little better for a couple of months. Laker isn't spending much time at home. He goes straight from school to the library and then gets back late in the evening. Rick might be on the road but he always phones Audrey from somewhere. They talk and talk. After Audrey gets off the phone she'll maybe see Laker standing by the refrigerator or heating up something in the microwave.

"Hi," she'll say and it's not the kind of greeting that invites conversation. Then she'll go watch TV or sit in her room, propped up on the king-size bed, doing the crosswords.

One time, around midnight, she wanders into the backyard and sits there for a couple of hours on the edge of the lawn chaise, her chin in her hands. She balances there, birdlike, staring into the dark at her flowers.

He remembers how, back in the days when she couldn't make it out of bed in the mornings, he appeared by her pillow with pictures he'd drawn for her; always something happy or funny, sometimes tracings from comic books that he'd fill in with fluorescent lime greens and poppy reds and orangy yellows, colors so brilliant his eyes actually watered all the while he was making them. She turned her face to him and smiled. She took his pictures and held them up like they were stained-glass windows with sunlight streaming through.

He decides maybe he should be doing things for her again. Maybe that would make a difference, because, like the old days, she really does seem kind of sad. He starts, whenever he has an evening off, to try and spend time with her.

"Mom," he says, "want me to make supper?" and then he makes it. Or he brings her little gifts.

But all she does is look at them and say, "Shouldn't you be out with your friends?" So then he goes to a movie, by himself. No big deal.

Later, he comes home and tells her he's gone with somebody. It's all pretty pathetic.

"Life sucks," he says to her one day, hoping that that will get her attention.

"Oh, it's just a phase you're going through," she tells him listlessly.

He goes to school, and girls always sit beside him—
one in particular, Sarah. He loves looking at her.
Loves smelling the warm scent of cinnamon that
rises from her fuzzy sweaters. "Hi," he says to her one
day outside school. It's snowing like crazy. Little
snowflakes fall and land on her lashes. "Hi," she says,
smiling back. "Want to do something?"

"Sure," he says, and she laughs, puts a mittened
hand in his, and leads him off to Rhonda's Video
Emporium, where they rent a wonderfully terrible
horror movie called *Bordello of Blood*. After that they
start seeing a lot of each other. Sarah lives with her
father, who, like Rick, is a long-distance trucker.

Christmas comes and goes. In January he gets his
driver's license. The night his mother and Rick tell
him she's pregnant, Valentine's Day, he relieves Rick
of the car and a half-full bottle of bourbon and goes
over to Sarah's house. They go to her TV room in
the basement. There, while she watches in amazement, he proceeds to get totally wasted. Sitting at the
edge of the couch, leaning toward him, her hands
tucked between her knees, her bare feet splayed out
to either side, she says, "Don't you want to talk about
this or something?"

Her face softly blurs, her makeup taking on an intriguing shadowy quality. Just before he passes out,
he tells her that she is the most beautiful angel he's

ever seen, while she eases her hand into his back
pocket and takes away his keys.

He gets home around seven the next morning.
Halfway up the back porch steps, he stops, kicks over
the geranium pot, mounded with gritty snow, because it annoys him and he feels like it. He then
walks into the kitchen, goes to the refrigerator,
opens it, and pulls out the orange juice container.
He drinks from it, drinks the whole goddamn thing,
and puts it back in the fridge. He turns to see Audrey
standing in the early-morning dusk like a saggy emp-
tied-out party balloon. She's been crying.

"Good morning, Mother," he says cheerfully, feeling like shit. He adds, meanly, "And what are you
doing up so early?"

Rick suddenly appears behind her, scrawny, hairy
body encased in a pair of black Jockey shorts. "You
can just stop it right there, buster," he says. "You're
lucky we didn't call the cops. You've got a piss-poor
attitude is all I can say. Either you get a grip or you
can get the hell out."

3 His last day of classes starts out with the usual charming scenario.

Rick, back home for three days, scowls in front of the TV. Audrey's head is bent over a cup of coffee, and she's carefully avoiding looking at Laker. In spite of everything, he thinks, she's still so blond and pretty.

"Why do you let him talk to you that way?" Laker says, appalled. "He comes home from one of his trips, and in five minutes he's got you crying. Why do you put up with it?"

"Laker, he's not a bad man." She puts her slender hand down flat on the table. "If you two could just get along a little better . . ." Her voice trails off.

He hesitantly reaches out and lightly places one finger on her back, tracing it tentatively down her shoulder. She stiffens. He lets his hand drop.

"I've got to go," he says. But he waits.

"Right," she says, looking into her cup, searching for whatever it is he can no longer give her. "So go," she adds.

"Why did you ever marry him? Mom?"

She turns up this stony face she's taken to giving him lately. "Laker," she says, "will you just go?"

"Fine," he says in disgust. "Fine, I'm going."

He picks up his backpack and leaves. He is late for school, again, and pissed off. But there is another element, a growing unease. Somehow his anger has blistered up against his heart like a burning coal. His breath only seems to fan it and make it hotter.

Later, when he comes home, he hears them arguing. Rick going on about how she forgot to get his beer when she was at the store.

"I just forgot," says his mother. "I'm sorry, okay?"

"Jesus, Audrey," he whines. "Didn't I ask you before you left? Just *before?*"

Laker walks into the kitchen. Rick is sagged over the table, chewing a sandwich. Chewing with his

mouth open. He actually makes noises when he eats.
This man is so beneath his mother, he should be beg-
ging at her feet for attention.

Instead, she's standing against the stove, her hand
on her stomach, on that obscene baby that will be
hers and his, drinking a glass of water. She quietly
finishes it, her pale throat arched like a Swedish
queen's. She sets the glass down on the counter and
says, "I know you're tired. I'll go back."

"Don't do that, Mom," says Laker.

She shoots him a look.

"I said," says Laker, standing between them in the
middle of the kitchen floor, "you don't have to go
back to the store. Mom, don't go."

"So why don't *you* go, hotshot?" says Rick, opening
his pack of cigarettes, flipping out the last one. "I'll
pay you five bucks if you go get me a six-pack of
beer."

"Screw you, asshole."

"Oh, right," says Rick, lighting his cigarette, ex-
haustedly shaking out the match. "Now he's calling
me an asshole. Nice son you raised, Audrey." He
picks up his sandwich with his other hand.

"I beg your pardon?" says Laker. "Don't talk to her
that way. And what makes you such a lord high shit
that you can make judgments on anything she does?"

"Laker, please," she pleads. "Stop this, right now."

"No, I mean it, Mom. He has no right. Look at him. Look at what you married. *Look . . . at him.* He has the manners of a pig."

"Pig?" Rick snorts. "That's nice, too. Oh, that's just peachy. Calling me a pig."

What makes that moment so different from all the others? The bright kitchen light. The floor that always gleams with a high fresh polish. Rick's terrified face, the sandwich dropping from his hand as their bodies collide. Laker on top of him on the floor, his hands on that whiskered chicken-skin neck. And then the banging and banging and banging of Rick's head on the black-and-white floor tiles.

Audrey has such thin arms. How does she manage to lift him off just like he was a five-year-old again?

Rick coughs and gags, his face scarlet. Audrey screams, "Get out! Get out of here! Get out of this house—get out!"

For a moment he hopes she means Rick. Then, unbelievably, he knows that she means him.

4 The bus depot in Duluth. His belongings bulging in a hastily stuffed khaki duffel bag. "A ticket," he says.

"Where to?"

He can't make a decision. He stands there, bag resting against his leg.

Heavy-lidded eyes look up: a quick bored appraisal, then back to the computer screen. "There's a bus going to Bemidji in fifteen."

"Fine. I'll take it."

The bus ride to Bemidji. There had been no time

to figure out what to bring along. But he did remember to pack Petey's whistle, still in its little pouch. It has hung over the mirror in his bedroom all this time, its bright stillness greeting him at the end of every day, reminding him of the Downeses and especially of Petey. He wonders what Petey looks like now. Eight months can make a difference in a little boy's life. He wonders if Petey even remembers all those great times they had together.

He'd also tossed in the journal that Sarah gave him for Christmas. Now, with two seats to himself, he pulls the duffel bag from under his feet and shoves it down next to him. He gets out the journal. It still smells like glue and new pages, and the cover is a deep purplish blue. He opens to the first page. His head hurts. He's shivering. The woman in front of him has taken off her wool jacket. The pen he's holding says Saint Jacques Animal Hospital. He has no recollection of where he got this pen.

He tries to think of something to write. No words come. There are no words deep enough to dig into all that he is feeling. He draws instead. A thin, dark sword along one edge of the page. Then he imagines the sword being driven right through Audrey's cold, miserable heart.

He wakes up, later, to see the night sky beyond the window. There are lonely stars of such brilliance.

He's never noticed before how many; countless stars, all twinkling and traveling in the void. You could get lost out there. They could suck you up and take you away. He feels dizzy, swallows nausea, and half an hour later he is in Bemidji.

TWO

Henry

Journal Entry: It's nighttime at the lake. Big bonfire on the beach—sticks crackling, and so much firelight that everyone's face is brilliant. The wind off the water smells like reeds and wet feathers. I'm with the old lady, the one who has named me for the lake. I'm sitting on her lap and she's pulling the melted soft center from a marshmallow and putting it in my mouth. Tonight she smells like wind and smoke. She has a soft sweater and I'm holding one corner, holding it on my face.

I Many times during the three weeks when he was on his own, he went into the white, pillared, plantation-style library on Beltrami Avenue. He sat and read plays. He read *A Streetcar Named Desire* three times. Between the covers there was a heartbeat, a life, a kind of understanding about how the world worked.

Many times during those three weeks, especially after his money ran out and he was relying on handouts, he thought of asking to work there at the library. Just for a while. The head librarian wore glasses with emerald frames. She was helpful and polite. She never kicked him out except at closing. Only her eyes held a searching quality that told him she knew. He was underage. A runaway. He had no address.

Many times, also, he went to the telephone booth at the waterfront, near Paul Bunyan's statue, and picked up the phone. He never could quite make that call home. The broken-down booth smelled of vomit, urine, and stale cigarette smoke, and even though he always left the door open, the combination—hinting at shabby despair and regret—was more than he could stand.

His dreams, whenever he slept, whenever he dreamed, bled into his waking life. Each new morning slipped him farther down. Shadows skittered across his path, lurked behind buildings and gathered along the blue fringes of shade trees. He knew that he, too, was becoming a shadow, living as he did at the edge of people's careless snacks and crisp plastic bags that held groceries, new shoes, medicine for their children. He avoided eye contact, remembered to stay back a distance when he begged for spare change. Most of all, he avoided the others who were shadows, too, who stood in doorways or slept in bruised and temporary stillness.

On a rainy morning under the Thriftway Drugs

canopy, an old man hands him an assortment of nickles and quarters and pennies. He remembers him from the day before; he'd given him money then, too.

Today the man complains about "the goddamn economy," "the goddamn weather," and his arthritis. "That's my daughter," he says, as a woman drives up. "My wife died just over two years ago and I've been henpecked ever since."

They drive away, but minutes later they're back. The car lurches to a halt. The two of them are arguing. The old man finally rolls down his window, studies Laker for one eternal moment while his daughter, behind the steering wheel, smokes and fumes and listens to the radio. Laker stands, shrunken and zipped and snapped and collared inside his damp, sweaty leather jacket, and then hears this unexpected question: "Do you do yard work?"

He's scared. He hesitates. But an offer is being made.

"Six dollars an hour. Cash. Name's Henry Olsen."

He gets into the cigarette-smelling car. Its heat and strange comfort shake up his whole being, making him churn and reel. He tries to focus on the bright images in the front seat. The daughter in eye-splitting turquoise. The old man in a green plaid, fedora-style hat and yellow slicker.

"And now, Vera Lynne," says Henry Olsen, "if it isn't too goddamn much trouble for you, I'd like you to drop us both off at my house."

"You're not serious," she says.

"I'm perfectly serious. This young man needs a bath and a hot meal, a place to sack out and some honest work."

"You can't do this," she whispers. "This is crazy. He'll rob you blind and murder you in your sleep. I can't allow this."

"Well, Vera Lynne, I still have a little free will. Although I must say, lately it's been shot through with holes." He turns stiffly to look at Laker. "Are you planning to murder me in my sleep?"

"No, sir," he says, horrified.

"And are you going to rob me blind?"

"No. No, sir. No, not at all."

The old man's face relaxes into a smile. He turns around again and says to the daughter, "See?"

The angry daughter drops them off. So, Laker wonders, is this guy an old pervert? Or is he just lonely as hell?

Then he's showering in this strange house, the hot water and the luxury of being clean and the gray fleece sweat suit Henry Olsen has lent him combining to make him wobbly with exhaustion. He emerges from the bathroom to see the old man standing by the stove wearing a chef's apron that says TRY A LITTLE TENDERNESS—THE PORK PRODUCERS. He's easing flour-dusted stuff into a pan and pointing off to the corner where the washing machine is and telling Laker that the work he has to offer him can wait until morning, and how does he feel about that?

"That would be fine," he says gratefully.

"Good. I figure tomorrow's soon enough. Everybody's always in such a goddamn hurry."

Along with his rain-soaked clothes, Laker throws everything from his duffel bag into the washing machine. Then he pours in a cup of detergent, closes the lid, and turns the dial to Wash. With an alarming rattle and a high-pitched whine, the machine suddenly shakes into action. He jumps back, afraid he's done something wrong. And then, surprisingly, it settles into a gentle churning cycle.

"Trouble with Vera Lynne is her blind obstinacy," says Henry Olsen, reflectively poking at the pan with a metal spatula. "She operates on the notion that anybody over seventy-five has nothing to contribute— not that she'd ever put it into so many words. No, no, she means to be kind. She'd blow your nose for you if you asked her. Works in a seniors' home. God help those poor old buggers over there. She's probably got them all organized into wheelchairs and diapers and songfests."

A buttery, peppery smell has begun to steam and bubble up. He continues, "Do you like panfried fish? Friend of mine, Frank Johanns, was up at Blackduck Lake yesterday. Best walleye in the world."

Laker straddles a kitchen chair, his arms folded along the smooth, curved, wooden back, and faces his host.

"Of course, I don't drive anymore," says Henry Olsen. "Had an accident last year. After that I figured, at eighty-two years of age, I'd had a pretty good run at it. Who wants to kill somebody just because you're too damn proud to know when it's time to give it up? I miss it, though. I surely do. Kissed off a good-size chunk of my independence, right then and there. Any that remains, my daughter is only too happy to take off my hands. Got your driver's license?"

"Yes," he says.

"Had it long?"

"A while."

"There's a few things I should know about you, son—like, for starters, your name."

He hesitates. "It's Laker." He pauses, and then he adds, "Wyatt."

"Your parents must really like basketball," responds Henry Olsen, quick as anything.

"My biological father does," he says, with a slow

smile. "Apparently I was conceived during an L.A. Lakers game."

"That a fact?" Henry Olsen chuckles, flipping over a crispy, golden chunk of walleye. "That's one game he didn't get to watch." He turns down the flame. "Does he still like basketball?"

A lie seems less complicated than the truth. So he makes up something around Reg, stepfather number one. "I don't know. He took off shortly after I was born. We hear from him once in a while. Never used to stay in any one place for too long. But I guess he's settling down now, because he's married and got a two-year-old kid." That last part is true. Reg had somehow managed to track down Audrey at Christmas and sent her one of those posed, family-photo, Have a Wonderful Year kind of greeting cards.

"So where's your mother living?"

"Duluth," says Laker, and right away he realizes he's been caught off guard. Henry Olsen is an old snake charmer.

"So you're not too far from home, then. Could always go back if you wanted to." He carefully dishes the fish onto a platter, then sets it in the oven.

Laker blinks at the bright blue kitchen floor.

Henry Olsen nods sympathetically. "Life is full of suffering, son. Suffering is normal. How old are you?"

Might as well tell him. Sooner or later he's going to charm everything out into the open, anyway. "I'm sixteen. I'll be seventeen in four months," he says, trying to work up a little enthusiasm.

"Seventeen." Henry Olsen considers this. He pulls a couple of plastic food containers from the fridge and says, "See, there's this big difference between us." He brings the containers to the table, leans over to set them down, then stiffly straightens up. "Unlike me, you've got a thousand more chances to start all over again with people."

Laker turns his head, resting his cheek on his arm. Beyond the kitchen's modern sliding glass door, a door oddly out of keeping with the rest of the house, is an enormous old oak tree. The sun has finally come out and slants late-afternoon gold down Bemidji's summer sky. Backlit, a thick, ancient-looking branch rises over the roof of Henry Olsen's house. Thinner leafy branches protrude downward. Dangling from one is a child's wool mitten. It's bright red and dripping with rain.

The telephone rings, a black wall phone by the doorway that leads into another room. Henry Olsen answers on the fourth ring.

"No, no," he's saying, "thanks for calling, but everything's just fine here. Yes . . . well, that's Vera Lynne for you. Sorry that she bothered you with this,

Frank. Ever since her mother died, her diligence on my behalf has become an increasing pain in the ass. But today it occurred to me that I still have a mind of my own, and I guess it's high time we had a discussion about that. By the way, the walleye looks terrific. Just cooked it up. Say, thanks again for bringing it around.

"Well, well," says Henry Olsen, coming to the table with the rest of their supper.

"Do you mind," says Laker, "if I make a phone call before we eat?"

"Yes, I mind," says Henry Olsen. He wears half glasses, and he does a quick study of Laker's face before he loads up his plate with two pieces of walleye, a big spoonful of potato salad, and some marinated vegetables. "You should never make a rash decision on an empty stomach," he explains. "What's your hurry?"

"I don't know," he mumbles.

"Well, if you don't know, then you don't need to hurry. Eat."

Laker listlessly cuts off a corner of walleye.

"When's the last time you had a decent meal?"

"I don't know," says Laker. "I guess it was yesterday. Or maybe the day before. I don't remember."

"Fish is supposed to be brain food. What grade are you in?"

"Going into my senior year in high school. I guess."

"Listen, son, when you call that mother of yours, will you let me talk to her?"

He stares at his plate, his hands resting at either side. His nervous fingers curl and uncurl. He hopes that Henry Olsen doesn't notice what a mess he's in, here at this table where kindness abounds.

Henry Olsen clears his throat, wipes his mouth with his napkin, then sets the napkin down. He reaches out a mottled, veiny hand and pats Laker's shoulder.

"Make your call, son," he says quietly.

So, he will. That's all he has to do. Tomorrow morning he could be back on the bus, heading home to Duluth. Maybe the old man will even lend him the bus fare.

Maybe things will be different this time. Maybe this time, her shell will crack and she'll step away, laughing, and something about him will please her. Her eyes will soften. Her arm will ride easily along his back.

He pushes away from the table, gets up, walks across Henry Olsen's kitchen to the phone. He dials the number.

When she picks up the phone, the cord at the other end makes a familiar clinking sound. This means she's in the kitchen. The cord has passed across the fruit bowl, which is usually empty. He's pulled her away from her own dinner. She accepts the collect call, and then says, "Laker, where are you?"

"I'm in Bemidji."

"You're in Bemidji."

"And I want to come home."

"Laker . . ." She pauses, seems unable to continue, then quickly: "Rick and I have talked this over." She pauses again.

"Mom? I want to come home."

Has she turned to look at Rick, her blond hair falling over one eye?

The cord clinks again, over the bowl—the one he gave her two Christmases ago. It's the only thing he's given her recently that she's set out for the world to see.

"Laker," she says softly, "you can't live at home anymore."

I can't live at home. *Can't* live at home. He feels an overwhelming all-over cold, as if he's standing in a freezer. He's so numb, he's not sure if he can open his mouth to speak, and then, unbelievably, he feels these words forming in his mouth, foreign words as if some stranger inside his body has taken over and is about to speak for him. "Oh, that's all right," he hears this new voice say. "I didn't expect to, anyway. I was just phoning to find out how you were and if you needed anything."

He remembers bringing her tissues whenever she cried, making her supper when she couldn't get out of bed, calling to say that she couldn't make it in to work again today. No, not today, but maybe tomorrow.

"Well, Mom," he says. "Mom," he says again, softly. "Mom . . . I'm going to go now."

There's just silence at her end. Maybe she's crying. Who knows? Maybe Rick is there with his arm around her, holding her up, supporting her in this decision they have made together.

"I'll be in touch," he promises, and for just a few seconds, he waits. He waits for her to stand up for him. To tell him that she loves him. To ask him to come back. To tell him that they can still work things out. None of these things happens. Then, as gently as a kiss, he sets the receiver back in its cradle.

He turns, comes back to the table, sits down.

"You can stay," says Henry Olsen firmly, then clears his throat, "for as long as it takes to get yourself together."

"That might be quite some time," Laker says quietly.

"I'm in no rush, son. Time is something I've got more of than I know what to do with."

The old man looks away, out the window. Laker

follows his gaze to where the red mitten moves in a
light wind. It spins one way, stops, then begins to un-
wind high in the arms of the huge old tree. He wonders about that bizarre, perfect little mitten. He
wonders how in the world it got there, and how it's
managed, this far, to keep hanging on.

2 Sometime the next morning he dreams that he's asleep and someone has stolen everything he owns, including his shoes. He's lying in the rain. His feet are bleeding. Blood flows from them like scarlet flowers, and a green gas like the kind they show in bad horror movies slowly rolls up the street.

He wakes with a huge, sucking gasp and wonders where he is. Then he remembers yesterday. Remembers whose house this is. Remembers, with a shattering ache, the call home to Audrey. If he were a

cartoon character, what the illustrator would show
right now, he thinks, is a human being lying on
his back with noticeable cracks forming all over his
body. Just dark, empty-looking cracks. And then the
legs would fall off. Then an arm. Then the chest
would crumble apart. He looks up at a fly that's
buzzing around the dusty ceiling light. With his one
remaining arm his character lifts a large gun and an-
nihilates it. The fly takes a very, very long time to kill,
and in the process the room is totally destroyed. It
feels great.

He doesn't remember falling asleep or having left
the light on all night. The room is airless. The blanket covering him smells faintly of lavender. Another
light, the lamp on the night table beside him, has a
fifties frilly white shade. This was once a girl's room.
Maybe even the daughter's. It depresses him to be in
what might have been, at one time, her bed. He sits
up at the edge of the bed and listens to the silent
house. He gets up, then pulls on the clothes he
washed the night before. Quietly, he opens the bedroom door and walks down the hallway and into the
kitchen.

"Morning," says Henry from behind a newspaper.
"There's orange juice in the refrigerator. Coffee on
the stove. Saved you some breakfast, in the oven.
Says here in our local newspaper that some genius

ran his truck into the lake and is now suing the city of Bemidji for improper signage. Isn't that just lovely. Can you imagine this poop suing the city? And they've got a dandy picture of him here, too, looking like a horse's ass."

Laker opens the oven door and finds a mound of pancakes on a plate, more than he can possibly eat.

"Here's another joyful tidbit. Some guy over near Hibbing, with an arsenal of guns, taking potshots at his neighbors. How goddamn charming. World's going to hell in a handbasket." He sets down the newspaper.

Laker comes to the table, sits down, pokes dispiritedly at his breakfast. "Did you sleep well?" Henry asks him. "That used to be Vera Lynne's bedroom."

"I figured."

Henry eyes the pancakes. Laker remembers to say, "Thanks. Thanks for the breakfast."

"Don't mention it," says Henry. "Those are buckwheat pancakes. Put hair on your chest." He laughs at his little joke.

The pancakes are very heavy. They have an odd, strong flavor. He doesn't know how he'll ever eat four.

"The yard work I talked to you about yesterday is, I hate to admit, beyond my capabilities. So stoke up." Henry goes back to reading his paper.

The yard work, in actual fact, is to be the demolition of an old but sturdily built shed.

"Built like a brick shit-house," Henry tells him. "Built it myself back in the fifties and built it to last. But nothing lasts in this world and I want more space to work in. So I need an entirely new kind of structure."

Laker eyes the building with gathering distrust. Then Henry starts in giving some very depressing directions: *everything* has to be removed and set outside into designated piles. The shed houses millions of totally useless items, from cans of rusty nails to dusty rolls of pink insulation. It's incredible. How do you designate junk?

"No, no," Henry says, an hour later, "don't put those sheets of sandpaper with the nails. Take them out and put them beside the picture frames. Oh, and those hooks, too. That way I'll know where they are when I need them. And there's a tube of Bondfast over in the corner there by the pail, see it? No, no, the glue. That's right. Put them all together. Good. And make sure you set them right by the tree where I can find them later. I'm working on those frames. That's my next project."

When Laker comes back into the shed, Henry asks, "Did you set them by the tree?"

"Yes," says Laker.

And, again, two minutes later, "You set them by the tree, didn't you?"

He can't believe how fussy this old guy is. How weighted down he is by all this junk. But he smiles, forms a question in his mind, and then asks, "Couldn't we just put everything out there and organize it later?"

"Can't do that," says Henry, with a frown. "No, no, no. Absolutely not. Far too confusing."

What's actually confusing is the parade of quirky decisions, like when Laker has to wrap three very ancient garden hoses into one coil and secure them with a good foot and a half of duct tape.

By late afternoon, Laker has pulled every last thing out of the old shed, organized it under sheets of plastic to keep out the weather, and bagged up several items that the old man finally admitted should go to the city dump. He's hot and itchy and covered with rusty grime. It's around that time that Vera Lynne drops by to see for herself if he is still there with her father. She parks in the back lane and stays in the car and occasionally impales Laker with a look, all the while talking to a girl who sits wordlessly in the passenger seat.

Henry, handing him a glass of water, says, "Prepare yourself. Vera Lynne is of the full opinion that you are an interloper. And by the way, that's my grand-daughter, Charlene, though you likely won't be granted an introduction. Not today at any rate."

He doesn't care to be introduced to her. Especially if she is anything like her extremely bossy mother.

Vera Lynne finally gets out of the car, leaving her door slightly ajar, and a manic sound rises up like Christmas bells gone crazy. The girl reaches over and shuts the door, rolls down her window, scowls at Laker, and fans a velvety, tanned hand at her grand-father, who smiles and waves back. Then she looks up into the enormous spread-armed oak tree. Laker wonders if the dangling red mitten is some kind of relic Henry has left there from her childhood.

Vera Lynne walks right past them, with barely a nod to her father, and goes, uninvited, into his house. About three minutes later she emerges with a plastic pail full of cleaning supplies, stomps past them, and gets into her car, slamming the door this time. She and the granddaughter lurch away.

"Stormy," says Henry. "Like a hurricane. And she'll take several days to blow out. Maybe then I can have that chat with her."

"You just let her walk into your house like that?" says Laker, staring at the dust that billows up behind the disappearing car.

Henry shrugs. "Used to be her house, too. And she

insists on cleaning it every week. Besides, you don't *let* Vera Lynne do anything. In case you haven't noticed, my daughter does pretty much as she pleases." He looks down at his feet, then raises his eyes again, directing his gaze at a place somewhere past Laker's shoulder. "Are you staying on for a couple of weeks, at least?" His eyes find Laker's again and stay there, level and unblinking. "Don't look so surprised, son," he adds softly. "What did you think I meant last night when I said you could stay?"

Last night he felt grateful, and if he were to look at that part of it closely, right at this very moment, he still is grateful. It's just that he is also beginning to wonder how complicated staying with Henry Olsen is going to become. But then there is that other alternative—the street. Again.

"What's wrong with your mother?" says Henry, his tone unmistakably sympathetic.

A wave of sadness and fear and regret immediately washes over him, making him catch his breath. "It's a long story," he replies. He hopes Henry doesn't ask that he tell it. He's not up to this. Not up for soulful confessions. He just wants to harden his heart. Besides, the most evident and terrible and shameful part of the story, the part where she told him she doesn't want him back, is all out in the open. And there is *nothing* he can do about that.

"What does she think you are?" Henry slowly wi away a corner of dust from his old Ford Taurus. "Does she think you're just some puppy that can be tossed away? Pardon me for being so blunt—but she needs her head examined. What happened? Well, I guess I shouldn't pry. I guess you don't want to tell me about it. Let's quit for the day and go inside the house and grab a sandwich."

After the sandwich Laker goes into Vera Lynne's old bedroom and lies down and sleeps like a dead man. He wakes up sometime in the middle of the night, throws open a couple of windows, and collapses back onto the bed and feels as if he is slowly sinking to the bottom of a very deep well.

*Journal Entry: The lake is right outside the window where I
sleep. At night it washes over the stones along the beach. I fall
asleep listening to that sound. Every morning I kneel on the
center of the bed and look out past the screen and smell the lake
and the flowers the old lady grows just below the window. Next,
I am eating berries from a tall bush. She has pulled down some
branches. "Help yourself, Laker," she says. She hums a little
song. Berries fall from her plump brown hand, plop down
inside a yellow pail, look like purple jewels. Soon the pail is
heavy with countless berries. They spill over the side, onto the
ground. "Leave those for the birds," she says.*

3   It just doesn't feel comfortable to be camping
in some stranger's house. Twice, the next
morning, he almost dials the Downeses. He
wants to talk to Gretel. She would probably understand. Maybe he could even go back to Minneapolis
for the rest of the summer. Then he thinks about
how people change. How things have a regular habit
of veering off in directions you never even thought
of. Who could have guessed, the morning they all
said good-bye to each other on the Downeses' front
street, that two years later his life would have come to

this. Who knew this would happen? *Trust the impon-*
derables, and things will work out, Mr. Downes had said.
Well, maybe Gretel wasn't even at Caravan Farm
Theater anymore. In the way that you obviously
couldn't trust the imponderables, she could be di-
vorced, or Mr. Downes's cancer could have come
back, or maybe they weren't even in Minneapolis.
Maybe they'd moved someplace else. Maybe Petey
had a little brother or sister by now, and Mr.
Downes's business had gone bankrupt and they were
all living in poverty. Anything could happen to people. And *that* was how the world worked.

He doesn't call. Instead, he helps himself to some
toast and juice and goes out to the backyard, where
Henry is already hard at work pulling siding off the
old shed.

"More of a challenge than I'd first imagined," he
says when he sees Laker. "Don't know yet what you've
decided. If you stick around, though, I'll pay you
your five dollars an hour. We have a gentlemen's
agreement, here, and I'm as good as my word—"

"Yesterday it was six bucks," Laker interjects.

"Did we agree on six?" says Henry, with a start.

"Yes. Yes, we did. We did agree on six."

"Seems a bit high. All right, then. We agreed. Oh,
and there's something else I want you to do for me.
First, how much do I owe you?"

"You owe me for six and a half hours of work."

Henry pulls a calculator out of his pocket.

"It's thirty-nine dollars," says Laker.

"Oh, of course." Henry looks embarrassed. "All this disorganization has put me in a muddle."

"That's okay," says Laker, feeling uncomfortable, wondering what Henry will do.

Henry pulls two twenty-dollar bills out of his wallet, presses them firmly into Laker's palm and says, "Keep the change. You've earned it. Now, about this car."

Laker says, "What do you want done?"

Parked beside the shed is Henry's thirteen-year-old Ford Taurus. Silvery gray, with balding tires, rust spots, and two broken door handles, it also has a dangling side-view mirror and a crumpled rear fender and broken taillight.

"Got to get it fixed," says Henry. "Even if I can't drive it anymore. Can't sell it the way it is. Besides, Charlene's got her eye on it. I never said, one way or the other, whether I'd give it to her. But I believe she kind of expects it. Although I'm not sure, now, what I want to do. At any rate, do you think you could drive it over to Blake's Auto Body and ask them to fix it up for me?"

"Sure. Whatever you like."

"Sometimes I wish I had never stopped driving. But then I had an accident last year."

"I know, you told me."

"Lost my confidence," Henry goes on. "Next February I'll be eighty-four. Who wants to give an old bugger like me his driver's license back? I'd have to go for testing and everything like that. No, I'm far better off this way. Besides, Vera Lynne's always here two minutes before I even think about needing a lift somewhere."

He drives the car over to Blake's Auto Body. Henry has called ahead to tell them all that he wants done. It's only a few blocks away. By the time he's ready to go back to Henry's it has started raining again. He waits half an hour, then decides to walk back even though the rain isn't easing up any. Soon he's soaked through and chilled.

As he walks he is thinking about what it would be like to be the loneliest man in the world. To be rocketed out into space all by himself. There he'd be, all alone, surrounded by the void—this big, vast, endless nothing. There would be no safe place for him except that rocket. Its thin walls would be all that would separate him from being lost forever in the eternity of time. He would know this, know it deeply with all of his spirit and mind, and it would frighten him. But soon, after a few years, which would just be heartbeats in the larger scale of things, he would forget about everything. He would forget about his family, his house, all the people he ever knew. Eventually he would even forget who he was. In fact, he might not even remember that he had once had a name.

Laker is getting closer to Henry's house. Then he stops, looks wildly all around him. This isn't Henry's street at all! What was the name of the street? What was the house number? He runs down the nearest alley, frantically looking ahead, then spots, to his relief, the top of Henry's monster oak tree. It's only one street over. He runs all the way to the house. Goes in the front door. In Vera Lynne's bedroom he peels down and pulls on dry clothing. He goes to the kitchen, looks out the window at the old man, who is still working in his backyard.

Henry has pulled more siding off the shed. He is out there with a wheelbarrow in this downpour, piling debris at the edge of his property near the back lane. At the rate he is going, there soon won't be any more work left to do.

Laker retreats into Vera Lynne's old bedroom, lies on her lousy bed. Rethinks yesterday's fantasy. The fly is no longer a fly, it's a cartoon parrot. It's up there on the ceiling lamp talking a mile a minute. It just doesn't shut up. It sounds just like Vera Lynne.

It's looking down at him, squacking and carrying on.
He lifts his gun. This gun is a very, very, very big gun.
It's a semiautomatic. He aims it at the parrot. Shoots.
The parrot explodes! Wonderful! Magic! Feathers
everywhere. Red and green and yellow, all floating
down around him. Landing softly on his pillow. He
gets off the bed, opens a Velcro pocket at the side of
his duffel bag, pulls out the little suede pouch with
the whistle. Goes back to bed, lays it across his chest,
feels like shit.

When Henry comes in, twenty minutes later, he is
still lying on the bed. Henry appears in the doorway
of the bedroom, toweling rain off his face and neck
and thick white hair. "Got the car off okay?"

"Yes," Laker says to the ceiling.

"You just going to lie there?"

"I was planning to get up."

But he closes his eyes and sinks into the mattress.
Behind his closed eyes he wills the old man to go
away.

"You know what I think?" says Henry. "I think
you're just lying there waiting for me to kick you
back out into the rain."

Laker holds his breath. He slides away. Feels a nice
numbing effect drift up his body. Feels no ache or
sorrow or anger. Numb is good.

Henry keeps standing there. At last he says, "Come

outside, now, and help me. Get up, son. Get up, now. We've got work to do. Work will make you forget your misery."

Laker wearily swings his legs off the bed and follows Henry into the rain. Henry goes at the rest of the work like a driven man. The walls fold in and the shed finally collapses. Puddles everywhere, soggy wood. Henry loads up one wheelbarrow after another with debris and Laker pushes each heavy load over the sodden ground and dumps it at the edge of the lane.

"Looks like we're done here," says Henry, at last. "My friend Frank promised me he'd come by with his truck tomorrow and cart all this stuff away."

It has finally stopped raining, and they go back inside and put on dry clothes. Henry, at the stove, makes himself a cup of instant coffee. His hands shake as he raises it to his mouth. "Goddamn arthritic joints," he says. "Golden years be damned. They are not golden. It's all a lie. Nobody ever tells you that getting old is hell."

Journal Entry: "Oh, my boy," she says, "just wait, later we'll have some pie. Go and bring in those berries." I am sitting on a high wooden stool. I climb down and toddle off outside. Outside her door I lift the pail, struggle with it back to the old lady. I feel important to be carrying the pail so full of purple berries. I won't let it down, won't drop it. I am grunting and talking to her as I bring it into the kitchen. She drops her knife onto the newspaper, beside the fish she's been cleaning, and she laughs and laughs as she watches me struggle toward her. Her shoulders shake. Her whole body shakes. I love that. I love it that I have made her laugh.

4 The following morning Laker wakes up to two voices in the kitchen, Henry's and another man's.

"Laker, this is my old friend and business partner," says Henry as Laker walks tentatively into the kitchen. "Ex-business partner," he amends. "Sold out to you, Frank—what was that, about ten years ago now?"

"That's right," says the man, standing up, extending his hand. "Frank Johanns."

"Hi," says Laker, reaching out his own hand.

Frank's grip is viselike; his smile, friendly. He looks to be about twenty years younger than Henry, with a hawklike nose, and graying hair that probably used to be black. He is a giant of a man who could give Paul Bunyan a run for his money.

"Understand you're staying with Henry for a while," says Frank.

"Yes," says Laker hesitantly. "A while."

"Well, you couldn't ask for a kinder fella," says Frank. "And that will include kicking your butt when you need it."

"I already found that out," says Laker, and the two older men laugh.

This is all I need, he thinks. An old boys' club.

A light rap comes at Henry's back door. "Will you get that for me, son?" he says with a smile.

"Sure," Laker mumbles.

Henry's granddaughter, Charlene, is at the other side of the door. She has an aureole of blond hair. Intense green eyes. Do they change color in different kinds of light? Some girls' eyes are like that. Her mouth is amazing. And she is in a very foul mood.

"Hi," he says, and then, "hi," again. Twice like that, just so she'll know he's an asshole.

She stings him with a sour look, narrowing her

eyes so that little witchy crinkles form at the corners,
just before she brushes past.

"Grampa!" she says, suddenly all sunny delight,
wrapping her arms around Henry, hugging him.

"Hello, my dear," says Henry with a huge smile.

"Well, well," says Frank, "every time I see you,
Charlene, you're a little bit older and a little bit pret-
tier. How's your mother?"

"Oh, she's fine," says Charlene. "You know." She
rolls her eyes.

"And to what do we owe this pleasure?" says Henry.
"Not that you ever have to have an excuse to come
and see me." His arm still rests protectively along her
back. "This young lady has always been my little
helper, Frank, did you know that?"

"Yup," says Frank, smiling at Charlene.

"But I bet you didn't know it was her who helped
me put in those back steps last summer. And you did
very well, didn't you, my dear."

"So what's happening outside?" says Charlene,
clearly offended by his patronizing tone. She pulls
away. "Where's the shed? And what's happened to
your car? Everything's disappeared."

Charlene goes outside with them and helps hoist
the shed debris onto the back of Frank's truck. As
if to prove to her grandfather that she can handle

anything he throws her way, she works harder than anybody. And not only is she annoyed that the shed has been taken down without her help, but she is unrelenting in her questions about the car.

"Are you sure Blake's will do a good job?"

"Yes, my dear, I'm certain of it."

"Well, are you going to sell it now, Grampa?"

"Not sure yet," says Henry. "It'll depend on how it all looks once it's done."

"I could have taken it over to Blake's for you. How come you're fixing it now? It's been over a year since you drove it. Are you planning to start driving again? Why do you need a car, all of a sudden?"

"Charlene," says Henry, with a private smile, "you ask too many questions."

She closes her mouth. Fumes silently for a moment. Opens it again. "So what about the new workshop? When are you going to build that?"

Laker decides he should give them some time alone. He can feel an intense dislike coming from her, and it is like being mentally stabbed with little swords by a gorgeous but angry goddess. He goes back inside the house, and a couple of minutes later Frank appears, goes to the sink, pours himself a glass of water, drinks it down, and says, "Looks like you've walked into a bit of a situation here."

"She'll be disappointed if he doesn't ask her to

help build the workshop," says Laker. Mad as hell, more to the point. He might as well give up right now. Henry's not going to offer him a couple of weeks more work, not if Charlene has her way.

"Henry's a little old-fashioned. He's never heard of women's lib. But he's crazy about her. I figure she could ask him for just about anything and he'd go for it. Well, here's my card," Frank says, handing him a red card that says LAKELAND LUMBER, FRANK JOHANNS, OWNER AND OPERATOR. The phone number, in black letters, is at the bottom.

"Call me," says Frank, to Laker's total surprise, "if you're serious about getting your life back on track. It isn't glamorous work. And the pay isn't anything to write home about. Up to you."

"I don't need to call you," says Laker. "When do I start?"

5 Frank was dead right: The pay's not a penny over minimum wage and the work is tedious and boring; loading and unloading trucks full of lumber, metal sheeting, unfinished doors and windows. His arms and back ache, and he works long hours. When he figures out what he'll be getting on his first paycheck, he knows that it won't be enough to move on; not nearly enough to cover a damage deposit and first month's rent out on his own somewhere. Frank picks him up every morning and drops him off every evening, which is a good thing because

Lakeland Lumber is way to hell and gone on the outskirts of town.

It is obvious that Charlene hasn't asked Henry if she could help build the new workshop: Some company puts up a tidy prefab job, metal siding, metal roof, four small windows. It is erected with amazing speed—three days.

After getting back from work on the fourth day, Laker goes out with the intention to at least offer to help put everything back in place. But he finds there isn't much left lying around the yard, just a pile of boards by the fence. It's six o'clock, and Henry is still in the workshop, puttering around.

"This is pretty nice," Laker says, entering the new space, with its new smells.

Henry is hanging up a row of hammers. He looks over at Laker, says nothing.

"I guess you're glad to have more room," Laker says, taking another stab at making conversation. After an awkward silence he ventures politely, "Out of curiosity, has your granddaughter been over to see this?"

"No," says Henry in a wounded tone, "Charlene is not speaking to me. And Vera Lynne finally left a half hour ago. Apparently I am incapable of rearranging all of this by myself. She threw out the hoses."

"Hoses? You mean all that old stuff I taped together for you?"

"Yes," says Henry hollowly. "Perfectly good hoses. Says she's going to buy me some new ones. I don't want new ones."

Laker wishes he didn't have to deal with this. He wonders what he's supposed to say. He wonders why Henry wouldn't just go out and retrieve the old ones.

"The old ones are gone," says Henry, reading his mind. "The garbage people came when she was still here and took them all away. Rubber hoses. You can't buy quality like that anymore."

"I'm sorry," Laker says. "About the hoses." And even though he isn't sorry about *them*—it actually seems pretty dumb to feel sentimental about garden hoses—what he really feels sorry about is that Vera Lynne must have known how Henry felt but threw them out anyway. It was simply a mean thing to do.

Then, all through dinner, Henry talks incessantly about the hoses. "She'll probably buy some cheap junk that will spring a leak in a month. Won't even last the goddamn summer. They just make junk these days. Absolute junk. You throw good money after bad. Those hoses were irreplaceable."

Later, as Laker tries to watch TV cartoons, to sink inside them, to feel invisible, Henry comes and sits

in the scratchy brown chair that matches the one
where Laker is sitting, swivels it around, leans forward, and says into his face, "I've had those hoses for
thirty years. Only one of them needed patching.
Perfectly good. Well, she's coming back tomorrow.
God knows what else she'll just toss away."

Laker, trying not to listen to him go on and on, is
now smiling like he *is* listening, not only listening
but totally engaged—you can do that as long as you
nod your head the odd time and *appear* to be inter-
ested—but all the time he is thinking, Okay . . . two
paychecks. Beginning of August. And then I'm out
of here.

So he hangs on. July is unseasonably cool. There's
a day or two of promising heat, and then the sky
clouds over and there's three or more days of chill-
ing rain. The lumberyard is greasy with mud. On his
break one day he comes shivering into Frank's office
to get a cup of coffee. His runners are soaked
through and have been for days. For two cents he'd
quit this lousy job.

"You need to buy proper work boots with steel
toes," Frank tells him, and his heart sinks. "They're
expensive, but you have to have them. Regulations."

"You didn't tell me anything like that when I
started here," Laker says, incredulous.

"Well, I'm telling you now," says Frank. "You'd

really be cryin' the blues if you got a broken foot from a falling two-by-four. And so would I. Payday is tomorrow."

The next day, after work, he asks Frank to drop him off at the bank at the corner, where he opens his meager account. Then he goes in search of the required boots. Standing in the middle of Wal-Mart, he makes the depressing discovery that even the cheapest steel-toed boots are expensive. He buys them anyway. He has no choice. With his purchase weighing him down, he walks to Henry's.

"Car's ready," says Henry unenthusiastically. He's still sitting in the brown chair. He's probably been there all day.

Laker stands over Henry for a couple of seconds, deliberating. "I'll go pick up the car," he finally says. Then, what the hell, he adds, "I'll come back and take you out to dinner. Would you like that?"

Henry doesn't even raise his eyes. "Eating out's a waste of money," he says.

"Come on, Henry. Let me treat you. Can't I at least do that?"

"You like fried chicken?"

He hates fried chicken, especially the commercial kind. He had his mouth set for a pepperoni pizza with double cheese.

"Henry," he says, "go and take a shower. I'll be

back before you know it. Then we'll go out and have
ourselves some chicken."

Blake's has done an amazing job on the car. The new silvery gray paint job gives off a soft gleam. They've even shampooed the upholstery. "Tell Henry he can just drop off the check anytime," says the service manager, handing Laker the bill in an envelope. "He's good for it," he adds. "He's one customer who won't stiff us. And by the way, I gave him a deal on those tires—thirty percent off. Sale's not until next month, but that's okay. Tell him Bernie said hi."

It turns out Charlene works at Chicken Palace where Henry decides they should go for dinner. She wears a white T-shirt and a short white skirt, and the way everything hugs her makes the rest of the tiny-bodied girls who wait tables look like a day at a kiddie play park.

"Hello, Charlene," says Henry, smiling at her.

"Hello, Grampa," she says politely, no smile. She leans across the table, wiping it with a cloth, and Laker can feel the heat rising off her body and smell her sweet musky perfume.

"We decided we would try dining at your fine establishment," says Henry. "What would you recommend tonight?" His eyes graze the menu. He looks up at her with a kind of twinkle.

"The chicken," she says, rolling her eyes, "is very good."

"Wonderful, my dear. We'll have some chicken. Two orders, please. Coffee for me."

"And you?" She turns stiffly to Laker. "To drink?"

Laker looks away. "Water. Please."

When she brings their order, she sets Henry's plate carefully in front of him. Laker's slides, somehow, up over his knife, knocking over his water glass. Water and ice cascade over the table's edge and into his lap. He's wearing beige pants. He looks down to see a dark stain spreading slowly up beyond his crotch.

"My God, I'm sorry," Charlene says, genuinely upset, and she whips off her apron and tries to catch some of the water with it. When that fails, she starts dabbing desperately at Laker's lap. "My God, let me get you another . . . napkin!" she says, rushing off.

"It's fine, really," Laker calls after her. "Don't worry about it. It's just water. It'll dry. Really. Don't worry." He is now sitting in a pool of water. He moves slightly. His pants make an embarrassing sucking sound. He doesn't know whether to get up or stay put.

Henry hands him his napkin. "See what you can do about the damage," he says mildly.

When Charlene comes back to the table, flushed,

handing Laker five more napkins, Henry says, "Now that we are all more or less on speaking terms, allow me to make some formal introductions. Charlene Taylor Sorenson, granddaughter, I would like you to meet Laker Wyatt, former street urchin and, whether you and your mother like it or not, my new boarder."

"Hi," says Charlene, and her face is all red, this time from anger. She turns quickly and walks off.

"Henry, we haven't even talked about me staying," Laker says, in low, horrified tones. "I thought—"

"We just did," Henry says gruffly, cutting into his chicken. "As of today I am charging you room and board. A monthly amount of . . ." He stops, deliberates, then names an amount that makes Laker's head reel.

When he finally comes up for air, eyes smarting, the old man's voice seems to be echoing back to him from a long, dark tunnel. He watches the mouth move as he envisions what will be left of his first paycheck. Not much.

". . . so you can make me out a check over the weekend," Henry is saying. "Or just give me cash, if you like. Cash, actually, is probably best for all concerned. As I said, that includes room and board, everything. You couldn't even get an apartment that cheap, much less buy groceries. This way you can save up a bit over the summer and still have enough to live on when you have to give up most of those good hours Frank's been giving you to go to school in the fall. Bemidji has a very good high school. Vera Lynne went there. And now Charlene." He pauses, adds, "I've given this a lot of thought, so what do you say?" and puts the forkful of chicken into his mouth.

Laker watches him chew. Watches his jaw work over the meat. The greasy smell of the place is settling around him like a dense fog. He is calculating how much this dinner will cost. He is speechless.

"You have to have an education," Henry continues, still chewing thoughtfully. He puts down his fork, leans in, nodding his head, patting the table with both hands. "And why not stay with me. You're sixteen years old—"

"*Seventeen,*" Laker interjects vehemently. "In *three* months!"

"You're a baby," says Henry, mildly. "You need time to grow up."

"I already am growing up," Laker says to the old man, barely controlling himself, just barely able to. "In case you didn't notice, I don't have any choice in the matter."

Henry helps himself to one of Laker's napkins, sits back, brings the napkin to his mouth, wipes it, lets his hand fall to the table, his movements slow,

deliberate. He turns his face to the window. Laker
catches a glimpse of it, the reflection of it, the deep
sadness of it, just before he throws down some money,
including a generous tip for Charlene, and leaves
Henry sitting alone inside Chicken Palace. He goes
out to the parking lot and waits in the car. He can't believe what just happened. Furthermore, he can't
believe that Henry would go and make an announce-
ment like that to his granddaughter—in public!
Whether you and your mother like it or not. What the hell
was that all about?

Ten minutes later Henry slowly makes his way out
of the building and gets into the passenger seat. He
sits there, deep in thought, with the door open, one
foot still outside on the white gravel. Finally he pulls
up the leg and, with some effort, drags his foot into
the car.

Laker sits, fuming, waiting for him to close the
door so he can finally start the engine.

"You forgot your change," Henry says, handing
him some silver coins and the five dollars that was
supposed to be Charlene's tip. "Well," he says, closing the door, "I guess we'll go now."

6 Henry's still in bed when Vera Lynne arrives at six o'clock the next morning. "I wanted to see you before you left for work," she says to Laker. "Come outside and talk to me where he won't hear us."

"Okay," he says, with a sinking feeling. He should be used to that downward plummet by now, it's becoming a regular thing, but he finds that he is never quite ready. So he follows her onto the back steps and manages, by the time they get there, to give her a good threatening scowl, even as his heart jumps into his throat.

She's a short woman. She takes her position. Leans against the wood railing, pulls her cotton sweater more snugly around her and says, alarmingly direct, "What's your situation at home?"

"I don't have a home," he tells her coldly, although he knows what she means.

"Are you going back?"

"I got kicked out." He stares back at her, daring her to take this any further, gathering his courage, feeling righteous anger rise.

"I see," she says, looking down at her shoes, then back at him. "You can't live here, you know. In case you're thinking you can just stay here as long as you want. I don't know if you know it, but my father is not a rich man. He can't keep supporting you, while you live here indefinitely. And he has been experiencing some . . . health problems."

"He seems pretty okay to me. For an old guy," says Laker, measuring his words. He's not about to tell her that last night, after Chicken Palace, they drove over to his bank, where he made a withdrawal, stuffed it all in a deposit envelope, and handed it over to Henry, leaving a grand total of twenty-three dollars and nine cents in his account. "He just wants to be left alone," he adds pointedly. Not that he really cares. Vera Lynne is quite welcome to bother Henry all she wants.

"Well," says Vera Lynne, her expression tight. She nods her head, smiles sarcastically. "You know nothing about him. Even if you think you do. You need to move on."

"I have absolutely no intention of doing that." Laker folds his arms across his chest. He can't believe this woman. "Looks like I'm stuck here for a while."

"Tell him," says Vera Lynne, as red fury rises up her neck, "that I'll be back tomorrow. It's our shopping day."

"Yeah. I'll do that. I'll tell him for you."

That night he notices that there actually *is* an unhealthy yellowish gray cast to Henry's skin. Laker hears him up at night, shuffling around in his worn-down slippers. No matter what time he wakes up, the lights are on and Henry is gargling in the bathroom, making old man sounds, or rattling around in the kitchen.

"Is Henry sick?" Laker asks Frank later. And then he tells him what Vera Lynne said.

"Near as I can tell there's nothing wrong with Henry—physically," says Frank. "You've seen the way he can work. He'll probably outlive us all. But he has

been out of sorts for a long time, ever since his wife
passed on. They were quite the couple, Henry and
Marianne. That whole family misses her, and they
seem to be doing a good job of driving one another
crazy. Grief will sometimes do that to people. Brings
out the worst in everybody. Takes a while to sort it all
out. So my guess is he's depressed. Not an uncom-
mon thing in old folks even at the best of times. And
Henry's been useful all his life. Now he doesn't feel
so useful. He doesn't fit in anyplace."

The next day is Laker's day off, and he figures he'll
offer to take Henry grocery shopping. He gets up
early enough to beat Vera Lynne at her own game.
When he makes his offer, Henry says, "That'll be
great. I'll just tell my daughter not to bother coming
over."

"I'll tell her for you," says Laker. "It's okay. I'll call
her. You go and get ready."

While he's waiting for Henry, Laker watches cartoons for a while, then flips to *Sesame Street*. Big Bird
and Maria are talking about family. What it means to
belong to a family. Big Bird is still the same crayon-
yellow giant he was when Laker was three. Even
Maria hasn't aged much. He wonders how they can
still look the same when all around them animals
have become extinct, rain forests have disappeared,
entire countries have been bombed and destroyed,

and every second of every day people's lives change disastrously with the wave of a cosmic hand.

It takes three quarters of an hour for Henry to finally emerge from his bedroom wearing what he always wears. But he has, thank God, already made out his shopping list. They get into the car and drive to Safeway, where Henry pulls out his pocket calculator and deliberates over every single item. He shambles up and down the aisles—each aisle twice, which makes absolutely no sense. At the checkout register he deliberates over pennies and nickles, and the sales clerk is smiling and helpful until, after slowly reaching into his back pocket, he discovers to his joy another whole load of silver and starts counting that out. Finally, they are all paid up and the groceries are bagged. The clerk has turned with relief to her next customer.

Henry exclaims, "Grapefruit! I forgot to buy grapefruit."

"I'll buy it," says Laker. "We'll go out to the car and I'll come back and get it. How many do you want?" he says, rushing Henry out the door.

"Pink," says Henry when they reach the car. He leans against the door. "Get the pink kind. Not the medium size. The large. Maybe I'd better go back myself."

"I'll go!" says Laker, flinging the groceries into the

backseat. "I know exactly what you want and I'll get you six."

"No, no, not that many," Henry says in alarm. "Here," he reaches for his back pocket.

"Don't worry about it. It's okay, Henry. I'll take care of it." Laker is already fleeing toward the store.

"Three," calls Henry behind him. "Unless, of course, they're very big, in which case I'll only need two."

This isn't the end of it. Henry has to stop by the drugstore, the bakery, the hardware store, and after that he tells Laker that he needs to get his hair cut.

The barber, thin as a reed, with some kind of an accent, maybe Vietnamese, greets them with, "Henry! Where is your daughter today?"

"Got a new chauffeur," Henry tells him, slumping into the chair. "Young fella's staying with me."

"Is that a fact?" The barber smiles at Laker. "Are you Henry's relation?"

Laker doesn't answer. Looks at himself, then the barber, then Henry, all flip-viewed in the wall of lighted mirrors. He is shocked to see that he doesn't really look like himself. His hair, for one thing, has grown quite long. He's forgotten when he last had it cut. "How much," he asks the barber, "for a buzz cut?"

"You want all that hair cut off?"

"Yes," says Laker. "I want a change."

"Okey-dokey," says the barber, solemnly. "Sometimes a change is good."

On their way back to Henry's, the old man keeps turning to look at him. Laker keeps stealing looks at himself, too, in the rearview mirror. It feels very weird to have almost no hair left. His face seems to be all eyes, now, and he looks strangely pious—like a haunted monk.

When they are almost there, Henry says, "Don't worry, son. It's handsome. Looks good on you. Shows off your features."

Laker is relieved but says nothing. He's thinking about his next paycheck. He is wondering how much he can save. When he calculates it in his mind, it still isn't enough. Not nearly enough to get a little place and be on his own. Maybe by the end of August. Yes, August. That'll have to be his new goal.

Vera Lynne's car is parked in Henry's driveway. Laker pulls up beside it, in front of the new workshop. He remembers, now, that he didn't call her. He sort of meant to, but he sort of didn't, either.

Vera Lynne has the stove all pulled apart, wire racks and chrome rings smelling strongly of cleaning fluids. Blue foam sinks in soft clouds down the inside of the oven. She turns from her work as Laker comes

in dangling four plastic bags of groceries from each
hand, Henry holding open the door for him.

Henry says to her, "You're cleaning," as if this is a most remarkable discovery.

"Yes, Dad, I'm cleaning. Or did you want me to stop doing that, too?"

"I forgot to phone her," says Laker, putting the groceries on the counter. "Do you want me to put these away?"

"You forgot?" says Henry. "Why did you forget?"

"I just forgot."

Henry shoots him a look that makes him feel both deeply uncomfortable and ashamed. "I'm sorry, Vera Lynne," Henry says, turning to her. "I should have made the call myself."

"I'll just clean up this stove and then I'll go," says Vera Lynne. "I'll get out of your way."

"Now, Vera Lynne," says Henry, in soothing tones. "You know that you don't have to do that."

"Yes, Dad. Yes, I do."

7 Every Tuesday after that, Laker faithfully takes Henry out to the drugstore or to get his hair cut or whatever little errand he wants to do. He especially dreads grocery shopping and has taken to hurrying on ahead, an aisle or so over, where he can pick up two or three items on Henry's list and then meet him back at the cart. One day, he's balancing bandages, a box of cereal, paper towels, a bag of apples, and a small can of shaving cream. He shoves the can in his pocket, not thinking

about what he's doing, just leaving his hands free to
pick up a box of economy-size no-name laundry detergent. This big guy comes up and says, "Were you
planning to pay for that?"

"What?"

"That," says the guy, indicating the orange cap of
the shaving cream that shows just above Laker's
pocket.

"Of course," he says, but it sounds like a lie. How
could he have been so stupid? Sales clerks think
every teenager is a potential delinquent. He is relieved to see Henry coming around with his cart. His
expression is both confused and mildly annoyed. He
hasn't seen them yet. He is lost in his inner battle,
juggling net weight with prices. His glasses are
smudged and need to be cleaned, so he's probably
not even able to focus properly.

"I'm with him," Laker tells the clerk. "I'm helping
him."

"Yeah, right," says the clerk who has probably been
working in groceries all his life and looks as if it is
something he has always detested.

Henry finally sees them and scowls at the clerk.
"You've gone and changed the labels on me again,"
he says, as if the clerk makes everything in the store.

"Is he with you?" demands the clerk.

Laker pulls the shaving cream out of his pocket.

"Don't put that in the cart until I've looked at it," says Henry.

"I wasn't stealing it," Laker tells the clerk as he passes the can to Henry. "I just ran out of hands."

"Yeah, a little five-finger discount," says the clerk, but he turns and walks away.

"Young man," Henry calls after his retreating balding head, "come back here and explain this to me. Why do we have to have aloe vera in shaving cream?"

The clerk pretends he doesn't hear him.

"Is he deaf?" says Henry.

"No," says Laker. "He just can't be bothered with us. We aren't in the big spenders group."

It hasn't taken many trips to the grocery store to figure out that the cost of a month's worth of groceries for two people, stacked up against the room and board he'd thought was outrageous, doesn't nearly make a halfway split. For his August room and board he even considers giving Henry an extra twenty-five dollars. But in the end he doesn't. You could buy a bus ticket for that much money. A bus ticket could get you to another place if you all of a sudden needed to leave the last one. If that's what you needed to do.

8 Sunday afternoon, end of August, Henry is outside digging up potatoes, beets, carrots, enough to feed a small army of starving children. In the past hour Vera Lynne has called three times. The last time, Henry told her, "Vera Lynne, I was at the goddamn doctor's last month. I don't need to go any more often than that. What? No, I don't need a ride to my eye examination on Tuesday. It's Laker's day off and he's offered to drive me. Yes. Yes, well . . . yes, come over and clean the house . . . of course. I would appreciate the help,

believe me . . . It isn't that. Very good, then. All right. I'll see you Wednesday."

"She's back at it again. Won't give me a moment's peace," Henry muttered when he got off the phone that last time.

Charlene comes over, parking Vera Lynne's car on the front street. She brings in a pot roast and some stewed vegetables. "Mom sent this. Peace offering," she says to Laker as they stand in the kitchen. Then she goes to the window, where she spies for a few seconds on her grandfather's labors.

"He doesn't want any help," says Laker.

"Oh," says Charlene.

"It's probably good for him, anyway."

"I know that," she says defensively.

"Your mom's called him three times today. What's up with that?"

"She's concerned!" says Charlene. "Can you blame her? My God, he's eighty-four years old."

"Eighty-three."

"What?"

"Eighty-three. He won't be eighty-four until February. That's six months away. Let's not rush things."

She shakes her head, glances away, then quickly glares back at him—this time with so much hostility he can almost feel the heat dancing off her pupils.

"He must really like you," she says. "I guess that's why you're still here."

"Hey! He's *your* grandfather, not mine," Laker counters. "And I'm not planning on staying any longer than I absolutely have to."

"Yeah, well," says Charlene, her shoulders slumping in defeat, "guess I'll go. Tell him I said hi."

He figures she must really love her grandfather to carry on like this, one minute pouty and angry, the next all red eyed and draggy mouthed. He can't help but watch as she trudges off to her mother's car on the street, gets inside, closes the door, and doesn't drive away, just sits all by herself.

He goes to the back of the house and sinks onto the steps that she and Henry built the previous summer. He runs his hand along the smooth railing, which is cedar and gives off a great smell whenever it rains. He thinks about his mom and Sundays before Rick came along. They had had these little rituals, nothing much, just stuff people do together when they feel comfortable, like watching special TV shows or eating cold pizza from the night before or playing cards. It dawns on him that before he came along, Henry and Charlene probably had their own rituals. He thinks about how probably being over here at Henry's provided her with a little refuge from Vera Lynne. He wanders back into the house, thinks about calling Audrey, hearing her voice, and just putting down the phone. But maybe Rick would answer, and he doesn't want to hear his voice. He looks out the living room window. Charlene is still out there.

When she sees him coming down the sidewalk, she starts up the car, but he is too quick for her; he has his hand on the passenger door before she can drive away. He opens the door, gets inside, closes the door fast.

She's startled. She swipes at her tears with the backs of her shirtsleeves, angry and embarrassed that he's caught her crying. Placing her hands on the steering wheel, she stares straight ahead.

"Look," he says. "If you want me to go and live someplace else . . . if that would make things easier for you and your family . . . I'll go right now. Just say the word and I'm out of here." He knows the minute he says it that he will. It won't be easy to live on his own. All he has to do is look at his bank account to know just how hard it will be. On lousy minimum wage. Never mind ever being able to go back to school. But maybe it *is* time to move on. Maybe that's what this conversation is all about.

"You'd do that?" she says, turning her face, her red eyes, to look at him.

"Absolutely." He locks eyes with her.

She sniffs. Takes a breath. "So how come you left home?"

"My stepfather and I had a—I guess you might say an altercation."

"And?"

"I lost my cool. Tried to throttle him."

"You tried to *kill* your stepfather?"

"Well, not actually kill—as in murder. I was whaling on him pretty good. I read somewhere that it takes quite a long time to actually strangle somebody to death," he adds, making a sick joke.

"Where did you read *that?*"

"My stepfather is a prick, Charlene," he interjects, with sudden anger. "Don't you get it? He was picking on my mom. She's pregnant. I'm not a violent person. You haven't got a clue of what it's like. You've got all these people who'd lay down their lives for you. . . ." His voice trails away. And you don't even appreciate them, he's thinking. You act like some stupid wounded little princess.

He wants to tell her to grow up. But he keeps staring at her, with his mouth shut. Finally she turns her eyes away.

"You don't have to go," she says at last.

He feels an unexpected wave of relief, as if he's been holding his breath for about two months, which in actual fact is about as long as he's been at Henry's. He draws in another long breath, and that makes him feel shaky. He can't trust himself to get out of the car just yet and stand on his two legs—not, at least, without immediately falling over. All along, he has to admit, he's been afraid of having to leave.

9 Over Vera Lynne's pot roast, he thinks about mentioning to Henry that he might want to go to school. He worries over what that might actually mean.

"Saturdays," Frank told him about a week ago when he'd made an inquiry about part-time work at Lakeland Lumber. He was just checking it out. In case. You never knew when you might find information like that useful. "You'd get your full day there," Frank continued. "I could also use some help late in the afternoon on Thursdays and Fridays. So maybe . . . thirteen, fourteen hours a week. That's about it. Just let me know."

It means giving up most of his wages, that's what going back to school means. It means absolutely no safety net if things here suddenly go wrong. And they could. He could wake up tomorrow morning and find Vera Lynne and Henry at the kitchen table, looking at him, having talked about him, having made some kind of a decision about him. You really couldn't trust anything.

"Penny for your thoughts," says Henry, peering at Laker over his half readers.

He envisions himself as some kind of small being curled up inside a floating blue bubble. The bubble carries him up to bounce along the ceiling. If the windows or a door were to open right now, he'd be gone. The wind would come and blow him away. There wouldn't be a thing he could do about it. Henry would eventually forget that he'd even been there. Nobody would know where he'd gone. Or that he'd been anywhere to be gone.

Henry says, "I've been meaning to tell you that I know the principal at our local high school very well. She's an old chum of Vera Lynne's. I had a little talk with her about you. She says you could come in to see her, if you like. Just for a chat. Nice lady. Mrs. Latifah Rose."

Laker nods agreeably, not saying anything.

At the end of their meal Henry brings it up again. Laker tries to avoid responding by going out and sitting on the back steps, where he can think. But Henry follows him. Hangs around with a cup of coffee in his hand. Repeats his comment about what a nice lady the principal is, as if it has escaped his memory that he had already said that part.

Henry then wanders off to his workshop. Comes back, mumbling to himself, trailing one of the fluorescent green hoses Vera Lynne bought for him. "The principal," he says, stopping in the middle of the yard like he's just had a new thought, "Mrs. Latifah Rose—did I tell you that that's her name? The principal? Unusual name. Friend of Vera Lynne's. Anyway, she's very nice. Very approachable."

"Right," says Laker, pressing his forehead against the cool cedar rail.

Mrs. Latifah Rose is a lady with a quick smile and a fondness for wearing orange. "Young man," she says the minute he sits down in her office, "Henry told me all about you. You've settled in there okay?"

"Yes," he says, feeling ill and hot. It's all he can do to keep from jumping up and leaving. But he'd finally promised Henry that he'd at least talk to her. He'd at least do that.

"Well, I just wanted to meet you before school started. I know that's a little unusual, but so is your situation." Her eyes are shiny, and she has millions of little braids all corn-rowed and then tied back with a satin scarf.

"I haven't made up my mind," he says. "I'm not sure what I'm going to do. I haven't made my decision yet."

"I see. And your mother is all right with you living with Mr. Olsen and everything? I have to ask because you are underage."

"She doesn't care. One way or the other. I haven't asked her opinion. Her opinion doesn't count anymore. Quite frankly it doesn't matter what she thinks. It's of no concern to anyone."

May Audrey rot in hell. He doesn't say that part out loud. He looks at Mrs. Latifah Rose's orange satin hair scarf. It falls along one shoulder like a rabbit ear. It strikes him as very funny. He looks away so he won't laugh. He doesn't want to offend her.

Mrs. Latifah Rose sighs. She swivels away in her chair, which is gray with tiny orangy red dots. She is looking out her window. Turning back again, she says softly, "Well, Mr. Wyatt. You may be underage, but everybody now is apparently expecting you to be a man. Especially, God help her, your mother. If you ever need somebody to talk to, don't hesitate to

come and see me. I mean that. You have *much* to
struggle with. Much, much more than you probably
fully understand."

Laker lowers his eyes so she won't notice how
trapped he feels, how utterly powerless. She begins,
delicately, to riffle through some papers on her desk.
He senses that this is to give him time to make some
kind of response. After a while he says, "I might
come here. I might try it. For a while. I'm not thinking of staying, you know. I don't know how long I'll
be here—" He stops, then adds, testing her, "I might
even be gone tomorrow."

"Mr. Wyatt, believe me, I'm leaving it entirely up to
you. It has to be your decision. All this has to come
from you."

On Sunday afternoon Charlene shows up to go with
Henry and Laker to a yard sale in the neighborhood.
Henry, Charlene tells him, really loves yard sales. She
chatters away as if nothing has ever been wrong, as if
everything between Henry and her has been absolutely fine for the past couple of months, like she
just walked out the door all smiles and came back in,
the very same way, five minutes later. Henry doesn't
even seem particularly surprised to see her.

"Grampa always manages to buy quite useful stuff,"
she says, as they wait by the shining Taurus for Henry

to finish whatever he's doing and finally appear. "He fixes it up and gives it away. He just loves puttering with all the old stuff."

He wonders briefly if she means the Taurus, too. If she still hopes that someday this fixed-up car will be hers. If she is just waiting for that day to come. He says, "Do you want to drive today?"

"Oh, sure," she says, too casually, and when Henry arrives, sauntering jauntily down the walkway to the car, Laker gets into the backseat right away so they can be in the front together. He figures it's the least he can do.

He watches the backs of their heads as they drive along, Henry's thick white hair, Charlene's tied-up, slightly damp golden hair. He can smell the shampoo she used this morning, the blossomy scent brought back to him on the wind from her open window, and he sees, for the first time, a tiny mole at the back of her neck, and along the ridge of her white T-shirt the soft gleam of a thin gold chain.

Later, at the sale, it's Charlene herself who is like a bloodhound, sniffing out all the old stuff, then giving her grandfather secret nudges. They get lost in their own little world. Laker feels that he should try to get caught up in the whole thing, too. But truthfully, he finds it depressing, seeing everybody out in

somebody else's backyard, pawing over their worn-
out personal things.

One box is marked Each Item One Dollar. In this
box is a pair of rusty metal earrings, a bracelet set
with fake jade, a couple of brooches, and a white
shell necklace identical to the one his father wore in
the one and only photograph he ever saw of him. It
gives him a jolt to see it. It's like having his father's
ghost walk right up and tap him on the shoulder. As
if some disembodied part of him just got up from
wherever the hell he is and floated off to Bemidji to
say hello.

It's a hot day, but Laker shivers violently and goes
back to the car to wait for Henry and Charlene. He
feels like just taking off. Then he hears Charlene
come up behind him.

"You disappeared," she says. "I never even heard
you go."

For one terrifying moment he feels as if he *is* disappearing. He quickly turns to look at her. Suddenly,
he desperately needs to see his own reflection. Even
if it's only staring back at him from Charlene's eyes.

She's smiling a carefully practiced smile, but it falls
away. "What's wrong?"

"It's nothing," Laker lies, drowning in her sea
green irises. "All that old stuff is kind of getting to
me, that's all. Henry's having a good time, though."

"He just bought a copper boiler for fifteen dollars. He'll probably take it back to his shed and polish it up and put some kind of varnish on it so it keeps its color, and then he'll give it away as a planter. That's what he did with the last one he bought." She holds out a clenched hand. "Guess what I bought you. I saw you looking at it." She opens her hand. Curled in her palm is the shell necklace. "I think it would look really cool on you. Do you like it?"

"It's . . . nice. Thanks."

She smiles. This time it's a beautiful smile. He watches her lips move as she says, "Let me put it on you, then."

So he lets her put the necklace around his neck. Feels her cool fingers fasten the clasp. But the necklace itself burns against his skin like a white-hot string of little coals.

Charlene looks so happy with her gift. "I'm sorry for the other day," she says. "I was just mad. Things have been pretty complicated. . . ."

"Charlene . . ." he says, pulling on the necklace, pulling it away from his skin, and then to his horror the strand holding all those burning beads comes away in his hand and everything goes flying off, bouncing against the curb and skittering between the wheels of Henry's car.

Charlene darts after the beads, scooping some up

as others roll away. She gets down on her hands and knees to retrieve some from the grass. Then, flat on her stomach, she reaches her long arm under the car. Laker watches helplessly the whole time, caught between gathering nausea and the excruciating urge to take off. A fiery ache climbs up his ankles, then comes to rest in his calves, until finally he bolts back to Henry's.

He goes into the bathroom, gets in the shower, turns it on full blast, sinks until he is crouched under the flying spray of steamy water.

Henry returns half an hour later. Laker has gone to bed. He hears a light rap on the bedroom door.

"Are you in there?" says Henry. "Can I come in?"

"Suit yourself," says Laker. "Whatever."

"I will, then, if that's all right."

Henry walks into the room, snaps on the light, comes and frowns at Laker. Then he goes to the window and looks out in the same manner as Mrs. Latifah Rose. "You're sliding away, son," he says, turning around. "I can see it in your eyes. And that's a bad thing. That's very bad. I don't know what to do with you. I really don't."

Laker feels a flicker of panic, sits up in bed. "I'm fine," he says. "You don't have to worry about what to do with me. Really. I'm just tired."

"Can I sit down, then?"

"I'm okay," Laker says hollowly.

Henry perches gingerly at the edge of Laker's bed. "What happened today? What happened back there with Charlene?"

"Nothing happened with Charlene."

"She gave you a gift. A necklace. You broke it and ran off like a fool. Now why would you do that, exactly?"

"Exactly?"

"Yes."

"It wasn't about the necklace . . . exactly."

"I see," says Henry, like he doesn't see. Not at all. In fact, he looks confused; his thick, wild brows practically knit themselves together.

Laker takes a breath, then blurts, "I only ever saw one picture of him. Of my dad."

"Your dad," Henry says, and then waits.

"And in it he's wearing this necklace. Identical to the one Charlene just gave me. Remember when I first met you and you asked where my father was? I told you how I got my name."

Henry seems to draw a blank.

"For the L.A. Lakers. Because I was conceived during an L.A. Lakers game. Don't you remember me telling you that?"

"Oh, yes, yes," Henry says vaguely.

"I said that we still hear from him from time to

time. But the person who keeps in touch with Audrey and me? That's her first husband. I found out about my actual dad one day when Audrey pulls out a picture of some person I've never seen before. Tells me *that's* him. I don't even know who this guy is. I'm staring at him. He's a total stranger. And he's wearing this necklace . . ." he trails away.

Henry thinks for a moment, then says, "Was he a mean son-of-a-bitch?"

Laker feels his mouth go suddenly dry. "Why do you say that?"

Henry slowly reaches into his pocket, pulls out the broken necklace string and several of the beads, looks sharply at Laker.

Laker feels sick. Is it true? Is that why Audrey never talked about him? He tells Henry, "She never mentioned him other than that one time. And maybe I don't want to know—if he was . . . like you said."

Henry nods his head, rubs his whiskers with his age-mottled hand. "This is going to sound peculiar, but someday you might want to know. Now, I'm going to put this away somewhere . . ."

"I just said. I *don't* want it."

"I heard you. I'm not deaf. Listen, son, you are going to have to find a way to pull yourself together. I understand you are in a fair amount of misery. I don't dispute that. But I'm an old man and I don't have the energy I once had for all this turmoil. So if you want to keep on being here, you are going to have to start trying a little harder. And that's just the way of it." Henry puts the necklace back into his pocket. He gets up and goes to the door. "Take a nap and rest your brain," he says before turning off the light. "I'll go make us some supper."

He misses supper. He sleeps all through that evening, waking only once, to look out at the empty, moonless night. When he finally gets up it's six o'clock Monday morning. First day at Bemidji's finest will start in a few hours.

He knows he shouldn't have left things to the last minute. Frank will take a very large strip off his hide for calling and telling him that he won't be in for work and that, without giving him any notice whatsoever, he has decided to go back to school.

"Don't you *ever* leave me short like this again," says Frank over the phone five minutes later, "or there will be hell to pay! You got that?"

"I meant to call you—last night."

"Doesn't matter. I can't have employees waltzing off to classes, leaving me with shipments going out and orders coming in and not enough bodies to handle everything. Why didn't you tell me before now?"

"I *did* tell you," Laker says, digging himself in a little deeper. "Sort of. I was thinking about going back.

Remember that day? I did ask you about it. So you did kind of know. That I might. That I was—sort of— thinking about it."

"Sort of thinking?" snorts Frank. "Well, then, think about this. You are damn lucky I don't just fire you on the spot. The only thing stopping me is that that would put Henry in a pickle. What the hell would he do with you then? He's already extended himself to the limit by having you there. Bending over backward till his head is touching the goddamn floor! Now, that's his business. But I owe him. That man has been my best friend in the most terrible of times. . . ." He pauses, takes a breath to calm himself. "So here's the deal. After school. Thursday. Four o'clock. Be here. And you sure as hell better not be late!"

Journal Entry: The smell of lake water is mixed with the smell of gasoline. I see a green motorboat. Now the old lady has laid a freshly killed fish on some newspaper. She's cutting it up. There's a lot of blood and a strong fishy smell. The smell gets all mixed up with a cut on somebody's hand. The hand is trembling. The cut is terrible, long and deep. Blood keeps flowing from the cut, dripping onto the floor. What floor? Not the floor of her cabin. This is another floor, another time. A cut hand. Cut hand.

10

There is a creative writing class for combined Juniors and Seniors. It's being offered for extra credit, which he can definitely use. When he called his old school in Duluth he discovered, none to his surprise, that he'll be repeating several eleventh-grade subjects. The writing course is run by his twelfth-grade English teacher, Mr. Pringle, on lunch breaks every Tuesday and Thursday.

On the first day in Pringle's creative writing class, Laker can't believe it when he sees Charlene, along with some other eleventh-grade students, come into the room. But of course you can't miss her, the hair, the skin, the roundness of her curves. Her lush peachy quality.

"Hi," he says, heart stopping, starting again, heat rising up his neck and into his face. He hasn't seen her since the necklace episode.

"Hello," she says coolly.

"So you're taking this class?" Stupid, dumb question. Of course she's taking the class. She's sitting right here, you fool, opening the wrapper on her BLT sandwich, waiting for everything to start.

"I'll get extra credits for English," says Charlene, looking at her sandwich, picking up half, taking a huge bite. She scarfs it down in three more bites. There are crumbs on her lower lip. She looks like a little girl. He wants to brush them away for her. Then he realizes that the thing he was just thinking, he is doing.

Charlene leans back in her seat like he's just held a lit match to her lip. That's it, he figures. She truly thinks I'm an asshole now.

Saturday night, when he gets back from working at Frank's, Charlene is there with Henry. She's curled up in the living room, on the sofa. Henry's in his chair with a TV table in front of him. They are chatting cozily and laughing—Henry's low rumble, Charlene's midrange giggle—and just finishing some take-home from Chicken Palace.

"You know that movie that Pringle told everybody they should rent?" says Charlene when she sees Laker. "I picked it up this afternoon. You want to watch it with me?"

What changed? Why is she being so friendly? "Sure," he says, uncertainly.

"We saved you some dinner," says Henry, merrily. He pushes away the little table, levering himself out of his chair. "You young folks watch your movie. I'm going to my room to lie down and read."

"Henry," Laker calls after him, "don't you want to watch it with us?"

Henry stops in the doorway to his bedroom, looks at Charlene, then at Laker, then back at Charlene.

Laker knows, right then, that they've been talking about him. It's so obvious. Their little looks back and forth.

"Grampa's tired," says Charlene, giving Henry a secret smile. "G'night, Grampa."

"Good night, dear," says Henry.

They watch the movie. It's a foreign film with English subtitles, called *Das Boot*. Laker has trouble

concentrating. He feels nervous about being alone 113
with Charlene. He doesn't like the fact that she and
Henry have been discussing him, maybe even talking
about the necklace episode. He especially doesn't
want to be some stupid-ass charity case that she now
has to feel sorry for.

After the movie Charlene hauls him out to the
back porch steps to sit under the stars. "See?" she
says, gazing up at them. "Isn't this nice? Smile, for
godsake. We're having a great time."

He can't tell her that being with her has the opposite effect of smiling. She's sitting so close that he
can actually feel the heat from her amazing body—
and it leaves him foggy-tongued and stunned.

She roots through her black canvas bag. It has a
picture of Shakespeare on one side and Black Island
Festival in big white letters on the other, and it immediately pierces him with homesickness for
Minneapolis and the Downeses.

"Oh, here it is." Charlene keeps her writing in a
spiral notebook with a deep purple cover. She flips
through the pages. He has always loved girls' hands.
Charlene's are long-fingered, her movements thought-
ful and quick. "Okay," she says, nervously glancing at
him, then back at the page. "I wanted to read this to
you. I just wrote it."

The Stranger
by Charlene Taylor Sorenson

He's some brief light
   Poised on the edge of darkness
   Poised on the edge of my dreams
   Poised on the edge of my knife
    Sharp
  So cruel
    So beautiful
  So precious to my sight

He feels weird the whole time she's reading it. He wonders if he is the stranger. And he feels as if he has been closely scrutinized. As if she has seen him in a way he doesn't even see himself. She finishes reading, and now she's looking at him, wanting his reaction. He doesn't know where to start. Doesn't like the way this makes him feel—all freaky and naked and edgy.

"You don't like my poem," she says at last, in a hurt voice.

"Oh, no, I like it. I just want you to . . . tell me about it."

"You hate my poem. Admit it."

"I don't hate your poem, Charlene."

She sits there, hugging her legs against her body,

big eyed, staring up at the night sky. After a while she rests her cheek on one knee. Shortly after that, she leaves.

He writes down their conversation in his creative writing notebook. He writes it all down, even her poem—what he can remember. A couple of days later he starts to think of it as a scene in a play. He rewrites it and then thinks maybe he'll show it to her. In the end he chickens out. Instead, he hands it in to Pringle as an assignment. He's changed around some of the details so that even if Pringle thinks it's good and asks him to read it out loud in class, Charlene won't recognize it.

He needn't have worried. Pringle hands back his scene with C+ written in red at the bottom of the page, and a note:

> This has reasonably good tension, which is why I'm giving you a passing mark. However, even though your piece seems to be about the unresolved feelings your characters have for each other, I sense that there is some deeper issue at play. D. Pringle.

Later, at Henry's, in Vera Lynne's old room, he lies on the bed and thinks about Charlene's poem. Her image of the knife gets mixed up with thoughts of his father. He wonders if he ever knew him and if he was a violent person. If, like Henry asked, he was a mean son-of-a-bitch—someone other than the character with the shell necklace and the strange smile and the cartoon balloon drawn over his head. But then why would somebody write "Hey, buddy! Where's my beer?" if he was anything other than just some ordinary guy? Nobody unusual or sinister. Maybe that's that. Maybe there just isn't anything to tell about good old dad other than the fact that he was a party animal who shacked up with Audrey for a while.

And here I am, he thinks, the happy result.

Journal Entry: The old woman is yelling at somebody. She's yelling at him to get out of her house. I'm clinging to her leg, watching all of this. A large, scary man is backing away. He points a finger at me, and I hide my eyes. But the old woman just stands like a bear, guarding me, until he leaves, until he walks out her door.

11

It's October. On the day of his seventeenth birthday he wakes up, goes to school, goes to classes. After school he takes the bus to the end of the route and walks the rest of the way to Lakeland Lumber. Later, around six-thirty, Frank, who is driving him back to Henry's, stares glumly at the magnificent Bemidji postcard sunset. One of his suppliers didn't deliver on time. He's got one hand on the steering wheel, the other on his gut. In between coffees, the guy pops stomach-acid pills. Laker doesn't even try to have a conversation with him. When Frank lets him off, he notices that Henry's car is gone. So is Henry. A note on the kitchen table reads: "Charlene's taken me to see that World War II movie. See you later. Henry."

He considers calling Audrey. Reminding her what day it is. His hand is on the phone. In the end he doesn't call. He finds an all-cartoon TV channel. For the next three hours he watches thievery, deceit, skulduggery, and general mayhem as gem-toned cartoon characters mouth off, blow each other up, run off cliffs, and get flattened by falling boulders, run over by cars, and defurred by exploding grenades or gun blasts down rabbit holes.

Now it's the beginning of November. He comes through the door after class. Henry, in the kitchen, says, "That mother of yours has sent a letter, finally. . . ."

Maybe it's a belated birthday card. He quickly pulls off his shoes, comes to the table with his jacket still on.

"Now, it's not for you," Henry warns heavily. "It's for me."

"*What?*"

"But she did send you something." He reaches into his pocket, pulls out a photograph. "She sent you this."

It's a picture of his half-assed baby brother. Written across the back: "Jeremy—a.k.a. Jem, at 1 month." Right then, he gets this sinking feeling in his gut that something is up. Henry has somehow been going behind his back to Audrey.

"Henry, what the hell is going on?"

Henry thinks for a moment, then says, "It's a private thing."

"*What's* a private thing? My life is a goddamn open book! I feel like I'm living in a frigging fishbowl!"

"Now that's enough of that," says Henry, firmly. "I will not have you raise your voice to me in my own house."

Laker stands. He's heard enough of this. He towers over the old man, clenches and unclenches his fists. He feels so much rage that another word from him and he swears to God he'll lose it.

Henry jerks back in his chair. There is an awkward twisting of his head. His jaw goes slack. Laker sees something in his eyes and knows instantly that it's fear and he has caused this fear. This makes him even angrier.

"Jesus, you just don't get it, do you!"

He slams out of the house, walks uptown, walks down to the shore, stares at the stars reflecting in the water from the black early November sky. Later, shivering, he walks back to Henry's. He doesn't talk to him, and he certainly doesn't feel that the old man deserves an apology.

For the next week he tries avoiding him, but no matter how late he arrives, there's Henry, waiting up in his brown chair, a small light precisely positioned to glow over his left shoulder. He comes through the door and Henry, raising his eyes from the page, clears his throat and says politely, "How was your evening?"

It can be frigging two o'clock in the morning and that's his greeting. Laker never says anything, never responds, until one night when it's been snowing and the streets are icy. He tells Henry, sardonically, "It was swell. Thank you."

"Wonderful," says Henry, without a trace of sarcasm. He coughs, sips away at a mug of steamy liquid. He looks shrunken in his ratty old bathrobe.

Laker stands looking at him, pissed off yet mildly concerned. "Are you sick?"

"I've caught a bug. Let's get to bed now."

The next day he comes home early. He's getting tired of staying out late, anyway. It's cold these nights. It has already snowed a couple of times. There's nowhere to go after all the coffee shops close. He is also badly in need of a good night's sleep.

He walks through the door and Henry greets him

with another letter. "This one," he says, holding it out, "is for you. I hope now you'll be staying in nights. Nothing can possibly be gained from prowling around like a cat in this crazy weather."

Audrey's handwriting on the envelope. A tiny wave of hope drifts across his heart.

The letter is short. His eyes race over her words. Her tone is cheerful. She and Rick and "Jem" are moving to Winnipeg, Canada. They have a dog now. Its name is Rex. It's brown and has woolly fur. It will be a good companion for the baby.

That's it. Not one how are you, how is your life going, who is this man you're staying with, are you safe, are you happy. None of that. No hint that she even wants to see him again. Just a cheerful letter you'd write to some distant relative you don't expect to be seeing anytime soon.

"Well, screw her," he says.

"Give it time," says Henry.

"No, Henry. Just screw her. Really. Here, you can read it yourself." He leaves the room with such force he knocks over a chair. He bangs into his bedroom and slams the door shut.

Later, much later, Henry quietly knocks. "Laker," he says, the door muffling his voice, "come out and have a cup of coffee with me."

"I don't really feel like it, Henry."

"I know that," says Henry wearily, and he coughs. His cold bug seems to be worse. "But do it anyway."

Laker comes out into the kitchen's glare. They sit at the table for a while, drinking coffee, neither of them saying a word, until finally he says, "I guess I have to tell you how I left home."

Henry nods encouragingly and sips his coffee.

He looks down at Henry's floor. "We had a fight. My stepfather was ordering my mother around. He's a bully. Next thing I knew I'd knocked him down and my hands were around his scrawny neck. That's when Mom kicked me out. It wasn't exactly one of my more stellar moves. But you know . . . she never stood up for me. She never did."

"Fair enough," says Henry. "Although Charlene already told me."

Laker lifts his head.

"Right around the time of the necklace incident. Well, just a little after. I wanted her to be a little nicer to you. We had a good talk. I haven't always gotten things right with her. Especially since her grandmother died. But I think I did this time. That's when she told me about that set-to with your stepfather."

"I was going to tell you—sometime," says Laker, shamed and betrayed and miserable.

"All I wanted, really, was to hear the truth from you. I'd guessed all along it had to be something like that. A final fight with somebody. Although you might honestly ask yourself who you were mad at. Your mother, as you say, never stood up for you. That's got to be tough to live with." Reaching into the pocket of his brown cardigan sweater, he tiredly fumbles around and finally comes up with an envelope. He places it carefully in front of Laker's cup. "In the spirit of coming clean with each other," he says, "I think you'd better read this."

Audrey's letter, the one she'd sent to Henry, contains Laker's birth certificate, which shows that he was, in actual fact, born in Canada in the very city where she and Rick are going to be living.

"Surprising world. I was born in Canada, too," says Henry. "Vast country. Oddly enough, Winnipeg is very close to the town where I grew up. Beautiful little place called Heron Lake. One of a chain of lakes in the Lacs des Placottes valley. Marianne and I summered there with our kids for years. Still have a little place there, although I haven't seen it in quite a while."

"She never told me I was born in Canada," says Laker. "I always thought it was Minneapolis."

"Seems there's a few things your mother hasn't bothered to tell you. Did you know, for instance, that your last name is Fontaine? Says right there on the birth certificate. See? Mother's name: Audrey Fontaine."

"Oh, that's nothing. That was Audrey's maiden name. Fontaine, before she got married to my step-father, whose name is Wyatt. But then my second stepfather is named Decker, so that's her name now, even though my last name is stil! Wyatt. I don't know what my father's name was."

Henry's eyes have glazed over with fatigue. "All these modern relationships," he says. "I find them very confusing. Well, you might as well go on and read what she says."

Written on a scrap of lined yellow paper, in Audrey's loopy, rounded handwriting, her note to Henry reads:

Dear Mr. Olsen,

The birth certificate is for Laker, because he should have it. You must think I'm a terrible person for moving up to Canada and leaving things the way they are. Thank you for calling me to let me know how Laker is getting along. You seem like a very good person. I'm glad he's settled in school and that there was no problem with the transfer. Thank you for taking care of that. I wish things were different. As I told you over the phone, my husband and I have tried to get through to Laker but we failed. I'm glad to know he's working and paying his way. I don't know what else to say. I never thought he and I would end up like this. Please keep in touch and call again if you need to. I'll send you our new address and phone number. I'm enclosing a picture of the new baby, as I thought he should know he has a brother.

Sincerely,
Audrey Decker

"You called her?"

"Seemed appropriate," says Henry.

"When?"

"The night you were so upset about that necklace Charlene gave you. Phone number wasn't hard to find. Weren't that many R. Deckers living in Duluth."

"Henry, why didn't you say something?"

"Couldn't see that knowing I'd called her would be of any help to you. You were so wounded and dead set against her. Can't say as I blame you. However, I also couldn't just stand by and watch you suffer and not make some attempt on your behalf. And that's all I'm going to say, right at the moment." He pulls a handkerchief out of his back pocket. Wipes his nose. Laker notices that his hand is trembling.

Reading Audrey's letter to Henry hasn't made him feel any better. It makes him feel worse. But try as he might, he can't stay angry with Henry, who, the more he thinks about it, is standing up for him in a way that Audrey never has.

Journal Entry: I feel an ache that is like nothing I can understand. When I'm hungry she feeds me. When I see her sitting by her window looking out at the lake, I run to her, put my head on her lap. Her hand always strokes my hair, my back. We are waiting. Always waiting. She sighs whenever she looks at me, touches me, picks me up, holds me. She sings to me, rocks me to sleep. But nothing touches the feeling. Nothing can soothe it. The feeling is an empty place.

There is a little stuffed bear. I can see it so clearly, the round, staring eyes, the brown fur, the pink felt tongue. And there is a bowl down by the beach. I put the bear into the bowl. Take it out again, put it back, take it out. She stands beside me, looks at me, looks at the water, looks at the empty sky. We are both waiting. This waiting feels as if it will never end.

12

Henry's cold drags on. For almost three weeks he's been coughing and out of sorts, and now, all of a sudden, it's something else.

As Laker's getting ready to go to school he finds Henry, in the early morning shadows, stretched out under a blanket in the living room.

"Went out to the kitchen last night to get a glass of water," Henry explains from the sofa. "Came in here for a while. Never left. Feel really tough. Hard to catch my breath."

"What's wrong?" says Laker. Is it his heart? Is Henry having a heart attack? His skin is flushed and blotchy.

"Weak as a kitten." Henry coughs. There is a deep rattle in his chest. "It's this cold, is all." He coughs again. Sounds like he's going to bring up a lung.

"Henry, do you have a fever? Where's your thermometer?"

"Bathroom. Top right shelf. Guess we'd better find out."

Laker stays home from school. He takes Henry's temperature every half hour, gives him orange juice, aspirin, cold cloths for his forehead. Nothing works.

Henry's temperature shoots up, and at ten o'clock he calls Vera Lynne.

"He's what?" she says.

"Running a fever," says Laker, trying to sound calm, holding the thermometer in his hand. He can't believe what he's reading. "It says . . . it's almost a hundred and four."

"I'll be right there," she says, slamming down the phone.

Henry has bronchial pneumonia. The doctor at emergency puts him on antibiotics that, Henry feebly protests, "look like horse pills." Two days later they bring him home and put him in his own bed.

That afternoon, in Henry's car, on their way to Thrifty's Drugs for more medicine, Charlene says to Laker, "Grampa's going to be fine. You heard what the doctor said."

"Another twenty-four hours, right? And then his fever should come down?"

"It's down already."

"I didn't know he'd get so sick."

"Nobody knew. How could we know? He had a cold."

Yes, he'd had a cold. But he thinks of all the times he could have made it easier for Henry, all the times he should have and didn't.

Later, after first Charlene leaves and then Vera Lynne, saying that she'll be back in less than an hour, he goes to ask if there is anything Henry wants. He's asleep. His breathing has an odd wheezing sound. Laker stands in the doorway and just looks at him. Looks at Henry sleeping. He can't believe how much weight he's lost. How sunken his cheeks are. Why didn't he notice this before? He looks into Henry's room. Realizes he's never seen it up close, only from a distance.

He walks in, turns around to see one wall that is completely filled with books. Incredible. He never even knew it was here. Amazing books. A complete collection of Ernest Hemingway. A thick tome called

PrairyErth by a guy named William Least Heat-Moon.
A book called *Fools Crow: Wisdom and Power.* Another
book called *The Solace of Open Spaces. Great Masters—
The Post-Impressionists* he lifts from the shelf. It opens
at a page filled with a painting by Paul Gauguin
called *Woman with a Mango.* The colors are dazzling.
Electric blue. Brilliant golden yellow. Skin tones of
the richest tropical brown. They make his eyes water.
Then, to his total dismay, he finds that he is standing
in the middle of Henry's room and he is crying.
Huge tears drop onto the beautiful book, splash
onto *Woman with a Mango.* He doesn't know why he
is crying. Worst thing of all is he just can't seem to
stop.

13

For the next three weeks, he sees Vera Lynne at least once a day. This in spite of the fact that between going to school and working for Frank there are plenty of hours when he isn't at Henry's. He takes care of things before he leaves in the morning, making sure that Henry has eaten and is warm and comfortable. Then he figures out something easy for lunch that Henry can heat up fast. He also makes sure all the dishes are done and things are tidy.

One day he gets back and there's Vera Lynne in

the kitchen. She's taken every single glass and cup and plate and bowl out of the cupboard. She's re-washing them. She turns to him as she briskly rubs a blue plate. There's this really pained martyr look on her face.

He goes into Henry's bedroom and finds him hiding behind his glasses, huddled up in the chair beside his bed reading a book called *Build Your Own Home in the Woods.*

Henry looks up, sees him, and relief floods his face. He whispers, "She's been here since just after eight o'clock this morning."

"Brutal," says Laker.

"See what you can do to get rid of her," says Henry. "In my weakened state she's wearing me down with all of her good intentions."

"Well," Laker says, still standing there, "maybe she'll just leave on her own. Doesn't she have a job to go to?"

Henry scowls at his watch, coughs, clears his throat, takes a sip of water, sets the glass down, wearily wipes his face with his hand. "Not for three more hours."

Laker sits at the end of Henry's bed. Reaches over to the incredible wall of books. Pulls down *Wolf Willow,* by Wallace Stegner.

"Wonderful book. You should read it," says Henry.

"Thanks. I will."

Two hours later Laker goes to see Vera Lynne out. She's pulling on her coat and boots and suddenly she looks at him and says, loud enough for Henry to hear, "This is a family matter. And you are not family. I've got nothing against you, personally. I want you to understand that. But it is *my* job to take care of him. Not yours."

Laker says nothing. He leaves her and goes into the kitchen and starts hauling out stuff for his and Henry's supper. If she's so goddamn concerned, why the hell doesn't she take care of him instead of washing clean dishes and making him crazy?

Henry is back in bed. Laker takes him soup and a grilled cheese with ham sandwich, and a glass of milk.

"Don't pay any attention to what Vera Lynne says," Henry tells him. "Don't let her make you feel that you don't belong here." He turns slightly on the pillow.

Laker lowers his head, then raises it again to meet the old man's steady gaze. It's a gaze that he now realizes he has come to count on, and that scares him. What would he do if anything happened to Henry? He takes a painful breath. He doesn't know what to say.

"Listen," says Henry. "I'm going to give you the

straight truth. That day when I brought you here, that was one of the lowest days of my life. It was exactly two years since my wife, since my Marianne . . . died. Anniversaries like that aren't exactly a spring vacation."

Laker nods.

Henry continues, "You need to know that my taking you in was, at first, partly a protest against my daughter's interfering ways. But now it's a sorrowful thing that you're getting caught in the cross fire between Vera Lynne and me. I can't see that situation improving anytime, not while you are living under this roof."

"That's okay," says Laker, feeling a flicker of panic. "I can take it. Really."

"Just don't be thinking that your being here has been a one-way street," Henry says, his voice breaking. He pauses, gathering in his dignity, and adds, "It's been a blessing in my life."

14

Near Christmas Henry is well enough to move around more, and he tells Laker that he has accepted an invitation for them both to go to Vera Lynne's for the holiday dinner.

"You're sure she invited me?" Laker asks Charlene a few hours later. They are sitting in Pringle's creative writing class, waiting for Pringle to show. He's always late.

"Mom's expecting Grampa to be there. And he told her you would be, too."

"Right."

"Come on," Charlene urges. "What else were you going to do?"

"I was planning on maybe a skiing holiday. In Switzerland. Working at Frank's is so glamorous. It has made me independently wealthy."

Charlene's face crumples into a smile. She starts to giggle. She turns around because Pringle has just come into the room, but she's still giggling. Her shoulders shake. He loves it that he has made her laugh.

During Henry's illness and gradual recovery she's been hanging out at his place more and more. Lately they've been sitting together for Pringle's class. Or they go to the library, where they pick out books they think Henry will get a kick out of.

He and Charlene drive to a Christmas tree lot and on Henry's instructions select a small balsam tree. They bring it into the house, all fragrant green bristles damp with melting snow. "Wonderful smell," says Henry. Somewhat wistfully, he adds, "Marianne always did like balsams."

"Remember those little crescent-moon cookies she used to make?" says Charlene. "Do you still have that recipe somewhere, Grampa? I could make you some."

Around that time a package arrives for Laker from

Mrs. Richard Decker—Audrey. From the size and shape of the parcel, it's probably an article of clothing. He doesn't bother taking off the brown paper wrapper. He leaves it lying around in the kitchen. A letter also arrives from her, with another picture of Jem. This letter is about as cheerful and dishonest as the first one she sent to him. This he also leaves lying around, with the invitation to Henry, "If you want to read it, be my guest."

"That *is* a fine-looking baby," says Henry, picking up Jem's picture, looking at it. "Do you think he bears any resemblance to you?"

Jem doesn't look like anybody in particular, just like any other plump kid at two months of age. But this second photo finds its way onto the fridge, alongside the first one that Henry tacked there with a Minnesota Pork Producers magnet.

It's kind of a low time, the way the festive season can sometimes be, and Charlene says, "What's up with you and Grampa? You're both so mopey."

"We're just as jolly as can be. It's a great time of year."

"Right," she says. "Well, I'm guessing that he's missing Grandma. And you, I guess . . . miss your mom?" She pauses, looks at him, and he looks away. "Laker, I don't want to sound like I'm telling you what to do, or anything, but . . . have you ever told her you're sorry?"

"For what? For her kicking me out? For turning her back on me?"

Charlene sighs. "Look, why don't you just call her?"

"I can't just call her. That's all. You don't know the situation."

"But why is she writing all of a sudden? Don't look at me like that. Your baby brother's pictures are on my grandfather's refrigerator. You think I don't know how bad you feel? I'm worried about you."

"Why?"

Charlene shakes her head in disbelief, doesn't answer.

"I have no idea why she's writing. Okay? I don't want to open all that up again. I'm tired of hoping. Of thinking she might change. It's just better to let things go. To let her go."

They are sitting on the carpet, leaning their backs against the sofa. Henry's Christmas tree, its flashing lights, makes little star patterns on her skin. He wishes he could turn to her and just hold her, but he can't. He doesn't know what she'd think. Doesn't know where it might lead.

Laker goes over to Paul Bunyan Mall and buys Henry a shirt. A thick, soft flannel in a bright blue plaid. It will look wonderful on him and keep him warm.

Then he buys Charlene a necklace made of tiny amethyst beads. He imagines putting it around her neck. Seeing the light catch the crystals. The V shape of the necklace resting against her skin. Then, walking past a gift shop window on Beltrami Avenue, he sees a small stuffed bear wearing a scarlet Santa hat. It's sitting on a bowl that is filled with colored glass balls. On impulse he goes into the store.

"That one's part of the display," the clerk tells him. "But we do have one other." She's in her early twenties. A brilliant silk scarf is tied at her throat, and her skirt is skin-tight black leather. He watches her walk away, her hips swaying almost imperceptibly as she goes and gets the other bear, brings it back to him. He takes it, smiles at her, then stares into the bear's face, its goofy brown eyes, at its pink tongue, the lopsided red hat. Something like memory shifts inside him.

"I'll take it," he tells her, and then realizes he didn't even ask the price. It isn't cheap, he discovers. The bear has a designer label. But it's too late now to tell her that he doesn't want it; his pride won't let him. So he pays for it and she tells him that the gift wrapping is complimentary and he chooses paper that is the exact vivid color of the first blades of spring grass. He'll find someone to send it to. Maybe Petey. Maybe even Jem.

In the spirit of Christmas he also buys a card. It is

an art print called "Last Flowers," done by a French painter in 1890. It shows a wintry garden and a beautiful woman shaking snow off roses and tucking them into the soft folds of her hooded dress. He decides to send the card to the Downeses. Gretel especially will love it.

He sends the card with just his signature and no message. But the green box sits in his room, beside the frilly white lamp on Vera Lynne's dresser.

He has started to pull in some pretty good marks. Even in the subjects that aren't repeats. Henry is thrilled—after Laker gets an A+ on an English term paper, he sits down and writes a letter to Laker's mother, congratulating her. He reads it aloud, and Laker, appalled, says, "Henry . . . you're not going to send this, are you?"

"I'm sorry," says Henry, abashed. "You should tell her yourself. It's high time she knew what a smart son she raised."

Christmas Eve Henry is getting ready to go to church with his family. "You're sure you don't want to come along?"

"No, thanks, Henry. You go. I'm not all that religious."

"Don't need to be," says Henry. "The music's nice." He struggles with his tie. He's still a little shaky. And his hands, the arthritic joints on his fingers, are red and swollen. "What a confounded invention," he mutters. "Some miserable so-and-so dreamed this up as a test for old people."

"Let me give it try," says Laker.

Henry talks away as he submits to Laker's knotting. "I saw a man once, on TV. A fool of about seventy-five. He jumped feet first off a diving board into a barrel of water. And the crowd went wild! Shouting and cheering. And the idiotic announcer calls him a vibrant man. As far as I could see, it was a stunning display of senility—"

"Henry," Laker breaks in. "I don't know if I can make it over to Vera Lynne's tomorrow, either."

"And why ever not?"

"I've come between you and your family enough. And you've been so good to me. Really. I'll just stay here. It's no big deal."

"Answer me this, then. Have you ever had a completely jolly Christmas?"

"Nope."

"Well, neither have I. And to tell you the truth, I'm looking forward to this one," says Henry, with a glint in his eye. "Family dinner at Vera Lynne's should be priceless. Better," he adds with a wink, "than jumping feet first into a barrel."

* * *

In the morning they open their presents together.
Henry loves his shirt. He goes off to his bedroom to
try it on and comes back checking the sleeve length,
which is perfect. "What a wonderful shade of blue,"
he remarks, pressing down the front with his fingers.
"Marianne always loved blue."

"There you go," says Laker. "Maybe she was watching over me as I picked it out."

"Maybe," says Henry. He pulls a handkerchief out
of his back pocket and wipes his nose. "Now go on
and open yours."

It looks like a book. Laker unties the ribbon and
pulls back the wrapping. Nestled inside is an anthol-
ogy of plays—all by Tennessee Williams—a handsome special edition, a red hardback with gold
lettering that includes *A Streetcar Named Desire.*

"Henry. This is amazing. How did you know?"

"I noticed you were always getting Williams plays
out of the library. Figured you should have a set of
your own."

Inside the cover he has written:

> *For each age is a dream that is dying,*
> *Or one that is coming to birth.*
> *—A. W. E. O'Shaughnessy*

To Laker Wyatt. With all good wishes, Henry Olsen.

Next Henry reaches behind the tree and pulls out Audrey's present, still in its brown paper outer wrapping. Laker's heart does a yo-yo flip.

"Feet first," Henry advises solemnly, handing it over.

It's a sweater. Heavy cable knit. Gray. Good looking. She probably paid a lot of money for it. The sleeves are about three inches short of his wrists.

"You've grown some since you've been here with me," says Henry. "She couldn't have known that."

Laker leaves it on anyway. Pushes up the sleeves and wears it all day.

They go over to Vera Lynne's and Don's place in the evening. Laker has never been over there for longer than ten or fifteen minutes at a time and is worried about how he's going to deal with spending an entire evening with them all together. Charlene greets Henry and him at the door in a long, silky, dark green dress that has a deep V neck. The smell of pumpkin pie and roasting turkey mixed with perfume rises around her. She has glossy, sparkly stuff on her eyes and lips. Her hair does this magical thing down one side of her face.

"Pretty as a picture," Henry says, giving her a hug.

Laker doesn't know where to look. Or what to say. He sets his and Henry's gifts on the front hall

table. Then he drops down to his shoes, unties the
laces.

Henry has already wandered off into the living room to see Charlene's father. "Hello, Donald," he booms. "And a Merry Christmas. What did Santa bring you?"

Suddenly, Charlene is crouched beside him. The sweet smell of her makes him dizzy. He looks at her hands. Enfolded in them is a very small present with tiny gold stars pasted on the wrapping. "I made you something," she says. "I hope that's okay. I hope *this* gift doesn't make you upset."

He finally meets her eyes. "I got something for you, too."

"You did? You want to go outside? Sit in Grampa's car?"

Laker stumbles back into his shoes. Charlene pulls on her jacket. They go shivering down Vera Lynne's front steps, from which every snowflake has been swept, and get into Henry's car.

"Don't turn on the ignition. They'll notice us," she says. "Okay, you first."

The present Charlene has made for him—a big sea blue chunk of turquoise with four elongated bone beads—is strung on a thin strip of soft leather.

"Do you like it?" she says.

He turns to her. "It's fantastic! I love it!"

"Oh, good," she says, all smiles. "Let me put it on you, then. I'll tie it. There. Don't pull on it, okay?" She giggles, settling back in her seat.

"Now you," he says with a grin, handing her her present.

"Okay," she says, and quickly pulls off the wrapping. He notices that her hands are trembling. He can't figure out if she is excited or just freezing. "Oh," she says, taking out the necklace. "Oh," she says again. And then she is silent, and then she looks at him and he sees that she is crying and for a moment his heart almost stops beating.

"This is just so . . . it's beautiful, Laker," she says, looking down at the necklace, again. Big tears plop onto her hand.

It seems the air around them has turned crystal bright with the fabulous light of snow and stars and street lamps and the glow of Christmas at the amber windows of every single house on Charlene's street. "Merry Christmas, Charlene," he says. Leaning over, he lightly kisses her cheek.

Later, Vera Lynne and Don give Henry a new snow shovel. He already has three others, resting inside his shed. "Well, well," says Henry. "This will be a very useful gift." He turns it over in a perplexed manner and jokes, "Especially if I don't make it to spring."

Vera Lynne, flushed and humorless from several glasses of wine, rises from her chair and announces, "Let's eat."

"And have you heard from your mother?" Don asks Laker solicitously, as they all go into the dining room.

"Yes, sir. She sent me a very nice present."

"Ah, good," says Don, with a faraway look. He is the kind of guy who always looks as if somebody has told the most terrific story and he just walked in at the end and missed it all.

The gray sweater Audrey sent Laker is far too heavy for the steamy house. The turquoise necklace, though, hidden under the sweater, resting against his skin, makes him feel steady and calm.

Vera Lynne has barely spoken a word to him. When he and Charlene came back inside the house, she said brusquely, "Charlene, come and help me," and then offered Laker, "Merry Christmas," with a tight, fake smile.

Once they're seated, Don presiding over the turkey, she asks Henry if he'll say grace. He obliges, and after that she downs her fourth large glass of wine, helps herself to more, and asks Laker, who is sitting right beside her, if he'd like a glass of wine, too. He hasn't touched alcohol since just before he got kicked out of his home.

"No, thanks," he says. "I'm not a drinker."

"Well, aren't you precious," says Vera Lynne. She dabs her mouth with her napkin. "I, myself, love to drink, as everyone here at this table will tell you. But only, of course, on special occasions." She raises her glass and toasts him.

"Mom, this all looks so good," Charlene says a little desperately. "I like yams."

"Yes. Yams are good," says Don. "And you put marshmallows on them this year. That's a new touch, isn't it."

"The show's on the road," Henry comments dryly. "Vera Lynne, if it's not too much trouble, pass me down your famous gravy."

Some of the gravy flows onto the table. Charlene jumps up, saying, "I'll go get a cloth." She leaves and doesn't come back.

Don shoves a forkful of sickly sweet, slightly burned yams into his mouth. Laker has just swallowed some of his own. He only took a small amount, but there still seems to be a long way to go.

"Charlene!" Vera Lynne calls in a semibellow.

"I'll go see what's keeping her," says Laker. He gets up too fast and Vera Lynne's dining-room chair topples over. He picks it up, mumbles sorry, then escapes to the kitchen.

Charlene leans against the sink. The hot water is on full blast. She turns around and sees him. Her hair is all wobbly from the steamy water. Her mascara is smudged. A gravy stain darkens the front of her dress. He stands there indecisive, confused, and utterly sorry for her. Twice, he opens his mouth to say something, then can't. She rubs at the stain on the front of her dress with a dishcloth, but that just makes it worse. Angrily, she throws down the cloth, leaves the kitchen, and goes sobbing up to her bedroom.

He goes back to the table, takes his place directly across from Henry, who gives him a halfhearted wink. In that moment he realizes Henry needs him to act normal. Here he is, Laker is thinking, sharing Christmas with me and his strange family; the dinner party is a mess, his daughter is drunk, his granddaughter is in hysterics, his son-in-law won't even lift his eyes from his plate.

So for the rest of the meal, Laker graciously compliments Vera Lynne on her cooking, cajoles Don into a conversation about cars, and generally makes the best of it, just the way he figures Henry wants him to. People perk up a little bit, especially Henry, who seems relieved and grateful, asking for second helpings of everything. Afterward Laker does the dishes while Vera Lynne, who has finally sobered up some, creeps upstairs to Charlene's room. He and Henry leave before either of them appear again.

Midnight. They are back at Henry's. It has begun to snow. Little ice pellets ping against the windows. Laker sips hot chocolate, rests it against his chest. Henry has pulled his brown cardigan sweater over his new blue flannel shirt. He carefully sets his own mug down on the coffee table.

"What's that?" Henry says, pointing to the grass green box that contains the bear with the Santa hat.

Laker has brought it out of the bedroom. Set it under the Christmas tree.

"It's a present," he says. "That I didn't mail."

"Ah. Sending it home, were you? I guess you've had a pretty odd Christmas."

He doesn't know what to say. Touches the necklace Charlene gave him, then finally, "Some of it was really good, Henry."

"Well," Henry says, "we won't include Vera Lynne in the good part." He picks up his mug again, slowly drinks from it, puts it down. He seems to be gathering his thoughts.

"She was awfully fond of her mother," Henry finally says. Just like that. Out of the blue. "I think in

some way she's never been able to come to terms
with losing her. But then I guess we're all in the same
boat. Charlene, too. We all miss Marianne."

On his dresser, Henry keeps a romantically youth-
ful black-and-white photograph of her. Laker knows
Henry picks it up and kisses it from time to time, because lately he's caught him at it when he didn't
think he was being watched. In the photo Marianne
is riding a bicycle, smiling and waving for the camera
seconds before she zooms out of the frame. She's
not much older than Charlene.

"I guess you loved her a lot," says Laker.

"She was the love of my life. Simple as that. Met
her just after the war. She was eighteen years old. I
was thirty-one. What a scandal!" He chuckles. Takes
his handkerchief out of his pocket. Blows his nose.
"Never would have happened, though, if it hadn't
been for circumstance. She was the widow of a young
man who died in my arms. War was a hell of a thing,
you know. Anyway, I went to see her. To pay my re-
spects, you understand. And that was it. You never
know where this life will take you."

It's so quiet and still, the only sounds are house
sounds: the hum of the refrigerator, the ticking of
the old standup clock in Henry's living room.
Outside, the wind rises and falls. An alder bush, one

that got caught in an ice storm in late fall but still has some of its leaves, scrapes and taps against the window pane.

"So a man died," says Laker. "And because of that you found Marianne."

"That's right," says Henry. "Life is full of those kinds of chance meetings, don't you think? I mean, what made you get on that bus in Duluth and come to Bemidji, of all places? And here we are now, sitting together, all this time later. Strange how things work out. Often bittersweet, but a constant marvel— wouldn't you say?"

Inch by inch you gain a little faith, Laker is thinking. You go back five steps. Then move ahead. Go back again. He turns his head to look out the window again. To look at the shining snow. To think about the mysteries of love.

Journal Entry: There is a little spot of blood on my teddy bear.
The spot grows to cover one entire eye. Then I see another spot,
on his stomach. Another on his foot. I try to brush the blood
away. It smears all over his fur. Then I notice blood on the floor,
near where I picked him up. A splatter here. A splatter falling
there. Falling to the floor. Blood fanning out in flower patterns.
Flowers everywhere. The sun is shining on everything in the
room, and it's quiet.

15

Laker goes to make a withdrawal at the bank machine. He discovers that he spent more money than he'd planned on, at Christmas. The room and board he pays Henry is due. He doesn't know where he'll get it. He thinks back to a few months ago, when he could have said within a couple of pennies how much he had in his account at all times. How could he have become so careless? What remains in his account is seventy-seven dollars and nine cents, not nearly enough to pay Henry, and his next paycheck isn't due for another week and a half.

He thinks about calling Audrey, seeing if maybe Rick could spring for the money. He tries to imagine her in her new house, in Winnipeg. He tries to remember her face. But the image floats high above his mind, then drifts farther and farther away. He wonders if that's sometimes the way Henry remembers Marianne. As someone who was once here and has now gone to some unreachable place.

Finally he decides to go and talk to Frank. He asks Henry if he can borrow the car, just for the day, because he's got some running around to do. Henry says, "Sure. Go on, take it."

He drives out to Lakeland Lumber before his first morning class and finds Frank in his office. Like Henry, Frank weighs down his life with historical clutter like antique spools and rusted saws. On his walls at least a dozen framed family photos go right back to a long-gone ancestor who hauled logs with a two-horse team.

It's always best to come right to the point with Frank, so Laker tells him, "I might not be able to pay Henry this month. And after everything he's done for me—"

"I'll advance you the money," Frank breaks in.

He'd been expecting, at the very least, a lecture. But Frank, looking concerned, adds, "You can work

it off in extra hours this summer. That is, if you're
staying until summer."

It isn't just that Frank is wanting to make sure Henry gets paid. No, there's something else. Some additional agitation.

Frank shakes his head, "Have you heard about Vera Lynne's latest?"

"What latest?"

"She's talking again," says Frank, "about wanting to get Henry into a home."

"*What?* What home? What do you mean? Henry's fine. When was this all decided?"

"I'm glad to see your reaction," says Frank, with a grim nod. "He still hasn't gained back his old fighting form. But hell, he could live another decade. Well, maybe not that long. But a couple more years, at least. Don't you think that's right? At *least* a couple, maybe even more, you never know about these things. One day they're healthy and the next they're not, you never know at that age. You never know, do you."

"No," says Laker, "I guess not," agreeing with him because Frank seems at a loss, repeating himself and strangely pained. He's never seen him like this.

Frank slaps his hand with agitation along the counter and continues, with difficulty, "I'd hate to see him have to move out of that house. He and Marianne shared that place for so many years. It would be the beginning of the end for him."

He sits with Charlene in the cafeteria at school. In front of her are an egg salad sandwich and blueberry yogurt. While he watches her eat, his own stomach churns with panic about Henry, but he's worried about offending her by asking the wrong question. Since Christmas her eyes always have dark circles under them. Whenever he's tried to get close, to find his way back inside that moment when they exchanged presents, she's reverted to her turtle routine, backing off, disappearing.

"Has your mom mentioned anything to you," he ventures cautiously, "about . . . well, wanting to put Henry into . . . a home?" He hates the sound of that phrase. Like you're trying to find a good place for some stray animal.

"How did you find out about that? Who told you?" she asks suspiciously.

"Frank," he says, looking at her, waiting, not pressing the issue. He picks up a glass of water, takes a sip, sets it down again. Waits some more. Fiddles with a paper napkin, fashions it into a dart. Glances up, glances away. Waits.

Charlene puts down her sandwich, pushes back

her hair, and finally says, "Mom's talked about getting Grampa into the place where she works ever since Gramma Marianne died. She says that he'd have good care there and she could keep an eye on him. We wouldn't always have to be worried about him falling down and hurting himself in the night. Stuff like that." She won't meet his eyes.

"Henry? Is she kidding? He's getting his strength back, Charlene. It's just taking him awhile, that's all."

"Well, that's not what she says."

Later, when he gets home, he comes right to the point with Henry.

"Oh, that's just Vera Lynne talking," Henry says. "Don't pay any attention to it."

"Henry, what exactly has she been saying?"

"Oh, you know Vera Lynne," Henry says evasively. "She's always got to have the upper hand. Always afraid life's going to run away on her."

Henry turns away to his window. It's freezing rain out there, an unexpected thaw. He digs his hands into his pockets and says, "I've been thinking about Heron Lake a great deal lately. I still have my summer place there. Just a little cabin that Marianne and I bought years ago, not long after Vera Lynne was born. Beautiful place. Overlooking that golden lake. Haven't been up there since the year before last and now Vera Lynne's asking if I shouldn't be thinking about selling that, too. It would be a hard thing. Lots of happy memories there. Before things started to slide away."

"Let me take you up there," Laker says suddenly. "This summer. We'll drive up to Canada. To your lake. Spend a couple of weeks. Maybe we could take Charlene with us. What do you say?"

Henry turns back from the window, looks doubtful. "You'd do that for me?"

"Absolutely."

"Would we tell Vera Lynne?"

"Not until the last minute. And let's wait to tell Charlene, okay? We'll ask her when the time is right. Don't you think that's best? Summer's a long way away. Anything could happen."

"Well, then," says Henry softly. "Well. That's a fine idea."

THREE

Heron Lake

Journal Entry: The cut hand moves toward me. And then I can clearly see that it is not the old lady's. It's Audrey's. Her bloody hand, her bloody leg, her body, all cut. She is crying. Kind of whimpering. Then she stops. She stops moving. The old woman comes to her. Her hands flutter all over Audrey's face. She is calling to her. Saying her name over and over and over. Audrey isn't answering. Her face is as white as a stone.

I "My friend Merry, from Heron Lake, called this afternoon," says Henry. "I was just thinking about her, too. It's been a long long time since we last talked. Imagine that. You could have knocked me over, I was so surprised." He's come in from the outside, a gardening knife in one hand, a handful of late-June roses in the other. Laker's just back from another day of working long summer hours at Frank's. "Which color do you prefer?" Henry asks him. "I thought I'd send a bouquet to Vera Lynne."

His roses are dark pink, bluish red, pale yellow, deep peach. Their sweet scent just about takes over his entire backyard. Henry always cuts a few and brings them into the house and sets them in a blue glass jar on the kitchen counter. These days he whistles or hums tunelessly, works a little bit in his garden, or just sits contentedly and rests and watches the summer sun and the rain with equal pleasure. Something is happening to him. Laker suspects it's Heron Lake. Now maybe something else has been added.

"So who's this Mary?" he asks in a teasing tone.

"M-E-R-R-Y, as in Christmas," Henry says. "And don't you go reading romance into this. She's just a friend. And a very good one."

"Henry," Laker laughs, on his way to the shower, "sometimes you kill me."

One night in early July he gets back all dusty and sunburned from Frank's to discover Charlene and Henry standing at the kitchen table, poring over a huge map they've pulled out of a cardboard tube. "This is an area map of Heron Lake." Henry flattens it with his hands. "Come and take a closer look." The lake is long and thin. "It's not very big, as lakes go," he continues. "Eleven miles long and about a mile and a half wide. But oh, the beauty of it. It sparkles like a little jewel. And its face changes with the weather. See at the north end, west side, in the hills there, that's the cottage. See it?"

"Yes," says Laker. He looks up to discover that both Henry and Charlene are staring at him. Henry's eyes are shining with excitement. Charlene's are unreadable.

"Charlene and I have been talking this over," says Henry, with a glance at his granddaughter. "I figured it was a good time to let her in on the deal. Let her figure out how she'll work it out with Vera Lynne and all. So how do the first two weeks in August sound?"

"Great," Laker says, adding carefully, "but how are you going to tell your mom, Charlene?"

"I'll figure that out," she says. Then, pointedly, "It would've been nice if I'd been included a little sooner."

"You and I have been through all of that," Henry says firmly. "Listen to me. You know how your mother is. If she'd gotten even a whiff of this any sooner, she would have found ways to make all our lives miserable. And being there, living with her all the time, you'd have gotten the brunt of it. Isn't that so?"

"Yes, I guess."

"We were waiting to tell you," says Laker, coming to

Henry's rescue. "We just had to make sure it was the right time. I think it's great that we're all going. I really mean that, Charlene. An adventure, right?"

Henry hugs her shoulders, kisses her cheek twice, then a third time. "Now, my dear, are you going to be able to get time off from your workplace?"

"That, at least, won't be a problem."

Laker has noticed that, like Henry, Charlene is changing in subtle little ways. A few nights later, when he goes to pick her up to bring her over to Henry's, she is arguing with Vera Lynne, actually standing up for herself.

"Mom, I don't want to hear about it," she says. "So don't tell me anymore. I mean it." She leaves Vera Lynne sitting morosely on the front steps, dangling a glass in her hand.

"I can't believe I just told my mother to grab a life, but I did," says Charlene when she gets inside the car. "She's going on about Grampa again, about how he doesn't have the energy he once had and how he's failing and how the writing's on the wall. She's so drippy and melodramatic I can't stand it. She's practically got him in the grave, for godsake."

However, when he asks if she's told Vera Lynne yet about going with them to Heron Lake, she tells him, "No, but I will, and don't look at me like that. I will. I said I was going to do it and I will. I'm telling her tomorrow."

He lets it ride. Doesn't bug her about it. He figures it'll happen eventually. Then, in the last week of July, it does. He picks her up again, and she gets in the car, leans her head back on the seat, rolls it toward him, and says, "Mom figured out that *somebody's* going to Heron Lake. She goes over there today to Grampa's, and he's got all his mail scattered around on the kitchen table and there's this letter from his friend at Heron Lake . . ."

"Merry?"

"Right."

"She was calling Henry about a month back. What's up with that?"

"She and Grampa and Gramma used to spend lots of time together at the lake. Never kept in touch in the winter, but when spring came along somebody'd make the first phone call, and after that there'd be a few letters back and forth, talking about all their little plans and stuff until my grandparents went there for the summer. It was like their ritual. But now, of course, as far as Mom is concerned, Grampa's given up going to the lake. So she's asking me, all suspicious, Why is Merry writing to your grandfather all of a sudden, do you know anything about this? Really accusing me, as if I've done something horrible. And so I just told her, flat out, I'm going to Heron Lake, Mom, with Laker and Grampa, and that's all there is to it. End of story."

"So now she's *really* pissed off."

"Of course! We all knew she would be. But I don't care. Let her be. It's none of her business what I do, especially if it's not hurting me or anybody else— what Grampa does with his life isn't up to her, either. After all, it's his life, isn't it? For however long he's got left."

Early next morning, to no one's surprise, Vera Lynne calls. They sit in the kitchen and wait for her.

"This is it," says Henry. "So I guess I'll have to smooth down her feathers."

"Henry," says Laker, "it's none of her business."

"Try telling that to Vera Lynne."

"Well, why don't you?"

Henry looks down at the floor and considers this. He wipes his hand over his face and gets up and slowly wanders off and comes back again and seems about to say something.

"Just do it, Henry."

Vera Lynne arrives and sits primly at the kitchen table. She waves away the coffee Henry offers. "I understand from Charlene," she says, "that you are planning to go up to Heron Lake."

"That is correct," says Henry, carefully lowering himself into the chair across the table from her.

"Charlene," Vera Lynne says, "will not be able to accompany you. She has to work."

This is a lie. Charlene already asked for the time off, and they gave her the full two weeks. So what the hell has happened? Well, Laker guesses he knows. She wasn't able to stand up to Vera Lynne, after all.

Henry brushes away some salt that has spilled on the tablecloth. He has to be disappointed, but he has enough class not to show it. Laker doesn't want to be anywhere near the table and leans instead, arms folded, against Henry's thirty-year-old kitchen range. The radio is on low, the way Henry likes it, and some announcer is doing a farm report.

"You know," says Vera Lynne, "nobody's been up to the cottage for quite a while, and that's something I think we need to talk about."

"Talk away," says Henry, narrowing his eyes, leaning back in his chair.

"Dad," she says, "you're not thinking about keeping it, are you? I thought we'd settled all that."

"Vera Lynne," says Henry patiently, "I'd like to remind you that, in the first place, it is not yours to decide what to do with. Not yet, at least. And in the second place, it was a dream on which your mother and I expended a great deal of money and emotional energy. Not only for the family, but for ourselves. Now, if you don't want it, that's one thing. But Heron Lake is my one remaining link with the country where I grew up and it still calls to me and I still want it. And," he adds, emotion quavering in his voice, "and I think Charlene does, too."

"Charlene," says Vera Lynne, with a small, deflating sigh, "is a young girl who very much loves her grandfather and wants to please him. You know that, Dad."

Laker leaves the kitchen. He figures he's hung around long enough. Henry and Vera Lynne can thrash it out without him. He goes outside, fumbles around in the mailbox. Among the bills and junk mail is a letter for him, from Audrey. He sits on the steps and holds it in his hand. It's a fat letter. He's scared to open it. He lifts it to his nose. Waits for a trace of home to appear, a scent, maybe. It doesn't. What did home smell like? All he can smell is the air around him. That and the trace of Henry's roses in the backyard. He sticks the letter in his pocket. He'll read it later.

When he returns to the kitchen, Vera Lynne is sitting there in the same immutable position as when he left. Henry, with unmasked tenderness, reaches over and squeezes her hand. What did he say to her? Laker comes around to face her and is amazed to see tears rolling down her cheeks. She quickly wipes them away and looks bitterly up at him.

"Dad was very, very sick last winter," she says, her voice still full of tears. "We might have lost him."

Laker knows that she does not include him in this "we."

"What will you do," says Vera Lynne, "so far away from home, if he gets sick again?"

"Stop fussing, Vera Lynne," Henry interjects tiredly. "We'll manage."

2 Audrey's letter is long and rambling. He skims it until he comes to the final paragraph:

So I've been wondering what are the chances of you coming up here and seeing if you like Winnipeg. I guess what I'm saying is maybe you'd like to try and live with us next year. I don't know what your plans are. I guess I'll just wait until I hear from you. Jem is growing every day. It would be nice for him to get to know his brother.

It isn't an apology. It isn't a letter saying she loves and misses him. It isn't even an offer that he feels he can trust, because it isn't really about him—it seems to be more about his brother. And it definitely isn't a letter that he is going to show to Henry.

3 Henry, out by the small two-wheeled trailer that he's hauled along behind the car for many summers, has packed up everything they could possibly use in two years. Slowly and meticulously he filled every corner. Laker stood by, first handing him things and then watching him rearrange them in every single box and bag. Air in the bags. That was a big one. Green garbage bags containing sheets and pillows and blankets. The air had to be pressed out

of each one. And you had to hold the bag tight, so
air wouldn't get inside before the twist tie went on.

Now there are these evil, heavy, oily, musty tarps
that have to be hauled out from the workshop. Each
one weighs about twenty-five pounds. Placed just so
over everything. There are also five lengths of rope.
Each one goes over the tarps in a certain way, with
Henry's painfully precise instructions. "Lash it over
that way. No, no. That one crisscrosses over, like that.
That's right." And they have to be tied down very
firmly, "so they won't come loose." Laker has to
watch Henry make endless endless sailor's knots.
Millions of them. God, and he has to pull really hard
on them, sweat beginning to form around his bushy,
tangled eyebrows.

Charlene is waiting at her house. She phoned last
night to say that Vera Lynne agreed to let her go with
them after all. When she told him, Laker's heart did
such a joyful flip that he started to babble, "You're
sure? What happened? What time are we picking you
up?"

"Laker," she said, "take a breath. I'll see you in the
morning."

He still can't believe it's true that she'll be going
with them, that Vera Lynne has allowed Henry and
him this gift. Henry, when he heard about it, just

nodded his head, and said "good" like he wasn't all that surprised.

Laker times the tarps. It takes twenty-six minutes to tie them down. He is afraid that if they don't leave soon, Vera Lynne will change her mind.

Now Henry wants him to get inside the car and "apply the brakes."

"But why?" says Laker. "We already checked the trailer lights when I hitched it up."

"Never hurts to check again," Henry says mildly. He's wearing the same brown pants as the day he picked Laker up off the street, with the same green plaid fedora-style hat pushed back on his head. Tucked into the pants is the shirt Laker bought him for Christmas; he wears that just about all the time.

"Well," says Henry at long last, standing back, admiring his morning's work, "I guess I'll call Charlene and let her know we've been held up here. We can have an early lunch now, and then we'll go. What's so funny?"

Doesn't even realize how absurd the last few hours have been and what a total eccentric he is. "It's nothing," Laker finally says, helpless laughter shaking his body. "Henry, it's all good. It's just fine. What do you want for lunch?"

* * *

The sun is high, blazing, and white hot by the time they roll into Charlene's driveway. Vera Lynne is out weeding her flowers and Don, with a white rag, is lovingly cleaning the engine of his iridescent blue Mercury Mountaineer.

Charlene leaves the house with a big smile, walking quickly toward Henry and him, her blond hair a cloud around her tanned, freckled face. She's hauling along four very stuffed duffel bags—the black one twice as big as the other three—and Laker mentally praises the sun or the moon or whatever pattern the stars were in that made Henry think to allow more trunk space than either of them thought she could ever need.

He takes the bags and shoves them in the trunk while she goes around enthusiastically hugging and kissing her parents good-bye, her grandfather hello.

Vera Lynne says to Henry, "I called that lawn service. They said they'd go to the cabin and cut the grass. The plumber is turning the water back on. He has that extra set of keys, so he'll send his daughter ahead to clean the cabin. You won't have to do a thing. Just enjoy yourself. All of you," she says with a red-eyed sweep that even includes, briefly, Laker.

"That was very nice of you, Vera Lynne," says

Henry, smiling at her. He reaches out, softly pats her cheek, and her eyes tear up again.

"Dad, call me the minute you get there, okay?"

"We'll be fine."

"Call me. Promise that you'll do that."

"I promise," says Henry. "I'm going to be fine. We'll all be fine."

Vera Lynne gives her father a long, brave hug, with several pats on the back.

"Hi," Charlene says to Laker. Then, "hi," one more time in case he didn't hear the first one.

4 Heron Lake. Sunrise over the water. Birds glide, wide winged, close to its liquid skin, pierce the surface, then soar high once more. Morning at Henry's cabin. Henry and Charlene dead asleep, unconscious, profoundly dreaming. Wind suddenly stirs the leaves.

The cabin, with its high windows, has a wide, green view of the lake, the thickly treed hills far on the other side. Beyond that are the grain fields they saw yesterday as they traveled, farm after farm that stretched over the land in a beautiful Manitoba tapestry. The road at last led over an escarpment and swung deep into the valley, the little village of Heron Lake, then toward the lake itself—a shining jewel, just as Henry had promised.

Last night, there was the sound of crickets and frogs. The vast, starry sky at midnight hung like another country over their heads and made him reel under its power. He couldn't take his eyes away. A pale crescent moon had risen over the lake. Henry pointed out the North Star, the Big Dipper, the Milky Way, a ghostly, dancing line of shimmering northern lights. Then he started reminiscing about the old days. "This place," he said, breathing deeply. "Being here. The years fall away."

Charlene gave him a quick smile, leaned forward, cradled her head in her hands. "Last time I was here to spend a whole entire summer, I was twelve. It was just before Gramma got sick. I remember so many summers here. As soon as we got here, I had this urge to make mud pies. I used to put grass in them and decorate them with wildflowers, remember? You and Gramma would pretend to eat them."

Henry laughed, reached over, took her hand, and squeezed it.

Laker's heart contracted. This history between them. Summers at the lake. Family stories told under the stars. He felt like an outsider. Yet it was so good

to be here, the fragrant night whispering around
them, the dense bush with its shadowy, fingering
trees, the sound of the dark lake washing over rocks
below, everything alive and magical and somehow
frightening in an overwhelming, dumbstruck way he
couldn't place in any manner that made sense.

He had finally ventured, cautiously, "It feels like
something's out there."

"Like you're being watched?" said Charlene. She
leaned toward her grandfather and said, "Yeah, I always feel that here."

Henry offered, with a little chuckle, "That's just
Mother Earth talking to you."

"Do you really believe that, Grampa?"

"More and more with every day." Henry sighed
gently. "Yes, more and more."

Yet in the midst of all this living beauty, something
else seemed to be waiting. Something inexplicable.
All night in the unfamiliar cabin, goose bumps had
shivered along his arms and legs as he tried to sleep.

Now he sits on the gray cedar rail on Henry's deck,
tracing through oak and towering birch the line of
white stones edging the water a couple of hundred
feet below. He gets off the railing. He is pulled down
to the lakeshore and, once there, stands looking at
the green water in amazement.

When he gets back, Charlene and Henry are

finally awake and she is making Henry's breakfast, an elaborate affair including a poached egg and two pieces of whole wheat toast and two strips of bacon. The bacon and the eggs always have to be on separate plates—the bacon on a *little* plate, what Henry calls a side plate. Both plates always have to be warmed in the oven first "so the food doesn't get cold." It makes no sense. Just another of Henry's little quirks that you get used to. Oh, and you always have to have napkins. If you don't, Henry will look helplessly around until you get him one.

"Are you joining us?" says Henry.

"No," Laker tells him. "I'm going to go and sit on the deck for a while."

"Very good," Henry beams. "You do that. Wherever the day takes you. That's what this place is all about."

The room that will be his for the next couple of weeks smells of cedar, like the rest of the cabin, and there are two little paintings of orangy red flowers on one wall. As he enters, he can still feel his unease from last night hovering there like a dank entity. He rifles through his duffel bag. Digs down through layers of socks and shorts and T-shirts and jeans. Can't find what he's looking for. Finally he dumps the whole thing on the bed, and there in the tangle of his possessions is the journal that Sarah gave him so long ago. He doesn't know what made him bring it along. He opens it now to the first page, where he drew the dagger on the bus on his way to Bemidji. He remembers, like a physical blow, what he was thinking at the moment he drew it. He flips through the pale blue pages of the book. Except for that one thing, the dagger, the pages are empty, spotless. He goes out to Henry's deck, sits on a lawn chair, and begins to write.

Journal Entry: In my dream the lake is golden—as if a skin of light is floating on its surface. There's a face beside mine as we bob around in the water—somebody I don't recognize. She's an old woman and she's very brown and her arms hold me, then raise me up. I'm real young, maybe one or two, and she calls me her Sunny Laker Boy. Laker, she says. That's what she names me: Laker. Audrey told me once that I wouldn't remember anything like that. How could I, because it's just a dream, she said, and besides, babies don't remember things.

5 It's been a strange reverie. Almost a trance. When he stops writing he discovers he has made a total of ten entries. After the part about Audrey and the knife wounds and the old woman, he can't think of anything else. It isn't like making something up. It's more like trying to see something that's beyond the corners of your vision. The picture started with the old woman.

"What old woman?" Audrey asked, tucking him into bed, handing him his teddy bear. He was maybe six or seven.

"I remember her," he said. "I was a baby. And she was nice. She sang to me."

"It was a dream," said Audrey.

After a while he'd stopped thinking about the old woman. She was in some distant, untouchable time. Almost the same as Audrey was now. Even if Audrey's letter did say to come and visit them, come and stay with them, it wasn't real. It wasn't a real offer. It was something Audrey imagined might happen, in some other time, in some perfect place.

A summer storm gathers darkly at the south end of the valley. Soon some pretty wild weather rolls in. The heat drops dramatically, and a cool, strong wind carries with it the smell of rain. He closes his journal and goes inside. He looks at the clock on the wall and can't believe that two hours have gone by.

Henry peers out at the rough, choppy water below. Charlene races to the breezeway, where the wind chime clangs alarm and the casement windows bang open and shut.

Below them the dark green lake whips up foam. A big sailboat is caught in the middle. Lowering the sails and resorting to his outboard motor, the sailor scuds home to shore. Rain begins to fall, large drops that darkly splatter the thirsty wood on Henry's gray cedar deck. Then a real deluge. Soon after, rain turns to hail—bigger and bigger balls of ice that bounce off the deck and railing, until that gradually subsides. Then the rain begins again—plonking on the metal roof, streaming from the eaves down the drainpipe—watery sounds everywhere.

A scratching comes from the breezeway, at the outside door. Something hurls itself against the cabin. The front wall actually trembles.

"Stay right where you are, both of you." Henry gets up from the table and walks with a kind of ambling, shuffling gait to the breezeway. There is silence. Then the door opens. Whatever was out there bursts through, its feet thudding, and appears in the living room—a wet, desperate dog, large and wolfish, wearing a metal choke collar with a red bandanna. One ear droops, the other stands straight up. It makes for Charlene, acting as if she's its long-lost friend.

"We have a visitor," Henry announces unnecessarily, making his way back to the living room.

"What a great dog!" says Charlene. "Where did you come from?" It has planted itself with a kind of goofy delicacy right at her feet.

Henry gets a bath towel, hands it to her, and she rubs the wet fur until it's fluffy and bristling. The dog's shy, happy eyes never leave her face. When she sits on the couch, it goes over and sits on her foot, looks back over its shoulder, floats a pink tongue over her tanned knee.

"I'm figuring that's Merry's dog," says Henry. "He was just a gangly pup last time I saw him. But I'd recognize that droopy ear anywhere."

The phone rings not more than thirty seconds later. "By gosh, it could be Merry now, looking for him," says Henry. "Unless, of course, it's Vera Lynne. Will you get that for me, son?"

Laker picks up the receiver and says hello.

The voice replying is clear, almost bell-like. "It's Merry. I saw your car pull in yesterday," she says, then pauses. "This *is* Henry's, isn't it?"

"Yes," he says. "I'm Laker Wyatt."

An intake of breath, that's all.

"I think your dog's here," he tells her.

Silence. Then, "I figured he might be. He always did like Henry." Then, "You say your name's Laker?"

"That's right," he says, startled. His head has begun to swim with a low irritating hum. He wonders if they have a bad connection. Her voice finally comes back clear again. "Well."

"I guess you want to talk to Henry," he says. "He's standing right here."

"Hello, Merry," Henry booms over the phone, as if she's deaf or a million miles away. "Yes, yes, we're all settled in and glad to be here. . . . Oh, you saw us come in last night, did you? Well, well, your eyes must be as sharp as ever."

When he gets off the phone he tells them, "I'm going to visit Merry after supper."

The weather has settled into a fine mist by the time Henry sets off, the dog leaping joyfully ahead. They open the kitchen window to watch his progress on the little gravel road beyond the rolling lawn. Charlene calls after him, "You're sure you don't want one of us to come along with you?"

He doesn't reply, just lifts his arm over his head and slowly disappears down the road.

At around ten o'clock the white stars come out and blaze trails up the vast night sky. Henry calls and says, "I'll be here just a little longer. Don't worry. Merry will lend me her flashlight."

They wait up, watching the stars, sitting under blankets, deck chairs pulled right together, talking. Charlene whispers as if the stars could hear them. "I wish he'd get home. If he's not back in an hour, I think we should go and get him."

"He'll be back. Relax. So, has Henry been holding out on us?"

"What do you mean?"

Laker chuckles. Doesn't say anything, just looks at her.

"Oh come on, are you kidding?" says Charlene. "Absolutely not! Grampa's known her for ten years,

at least. She was always bringing stuff over that last
summer when Gramma was so sick. Do you know
that Mom got really indignant when I told her they
were spending some time together? You wouldn't believe it. I was sorry I even mentioned it."

Henry trudges back up the hill about a half hour
later. He walks into the living room and peeks at
them through the screen on the deck door. "Hello,
you two," he gasps. Then he has a fit of coughing. He
catches his breath and adds, "What a fine night."

"Grampa, are you okay?"

"Big walk," he says, still wheezing. "Well, I'm going
to bed now."

"Did you have a nice time?""

"Very." Henry walks away. Ten minutes later they
hear him whistling.

6 This morning he opened his eyes to shimmering oak leaves beyond the summer screens. A fleeting shadow darted across his vision, hummed, hovered, dove away, darted back, hovering again—a hummingbird with a red throat and a tiny, stabbing beak. It was looking right at him, its wings blurring with movement. Then it vanished like a dream. He groaned, turned over onto his stomach, and melted back into the mattress.

Now he sits on the deck, in the full morning sunlight, with a cup of Charlene's potent coffee and his journal. He reads over the entries he wrote yester-

day. Thinks about what else he might write. But
nothing edges into his consciousness.

"Can I read it?" says Charlene. "What you've already written? You were so intense out there on the
deck yesterday that I figure it must be something really good."

"I'm not sure what it is yet," says Laker evasively.
He really doesn't want to show it to her. She'll probably think he's a psycho, writing such weird stuff. And
he *doesn't* know yet what it is. That part is totally true.

Charlene picks the binoculars up from the deck.
"Remember that terrific monologue you wrote last
winter? I was so impressed."

"Which monologue?"

"The one where you talked about loneliness.
About being the loneliest man in the world. It just so
amazed me that you had the guts to read all those
feelings right out loud."

Blushing, she quickly lifts the binoculars and
trains them on the lake below. For the past half hour,
now, she's been spying on Henry and Merry, who are
out in Merry's boat in the middle of the still, glassy
water, fishing.

"Do you suppose they ought to be out there like
that?" says Charlene, putting down the binoculars,
avoiding his eyes. "What if we get another storm?"

Laker stares at her. He can hear the slightest tinge

of Vera Lynne in her voice. She's also still blushing, and he doesn't think he's ever seen another person in his life who looks as adorable as Charlene does right at this moment.

"But I suppose it's okay," she continues, getting redder and redder. "Here." She hands him the binoculars. "Will you please take a look at them?"

He'd much rather look at Charlene, but he takes the binoculars anyway and trains them on Merry's small, duck green boat. As soon as everything comes into focus, Merry spies him spying on them and lifts her arm and smiles and laughs and waves and waves. She turns and says something to Henry, who looks up the hill, raises an arm, then lowers it, turning his face away. Something in that movement is so wistful and strangely private that Laker leaves him alone, turning the binoculars, instead, back on Merry and the sparkling water around the boat. The sunlight glows on her skin—immediately he thinks of *Woman with a Mango,* the Gauguin painting from Henry's book last winter.

"She's Cree," explains Charlene. "Or Ojibway. Well, maybe it's both. Maybe that's why I'm remembering it that way. Anyway, she even taught me a few words. Like the name of her dog, Tansi? It means hello. But I've forgotten the other words she taught me. I just remember being with her. That part is real

clear. Little things. Like her kitchen, for instance.
The berry jam she used to make. I was seven or eight
when she came to live here. She's got a beautiful
place. What are you staring at for so long?"

A flock of pelicans has just flown over their heads,
powerful wings beating out a long, low, heart-stop-
ping sound. There are seven in all. The first one
reaches a blue point directly over Merry, and the rest
are moving like thunderclouds toward her.

By around five o'clock in the afternoon Henry and
Merry are no longer visible on the lake. Maybe they
went back to her cottage. Time goes on and still no
Henry. Charlene says, "This is so totally unlike him."

Over the phone, about an hour later, Henry in-
quires, "Are you two young folks okay?"

"Absolutely," says Laker. "Where are you, Henry?"

"Oh, I'm still at Merry's. Just a minute. . . ."

Laker hears the muffled sounds of some discussion. Then Henry is back. "We're going to have a late
supper together." He pauses. "Would you care to join
us?"

"Don't worry about us. Charlene and I will find
something."

"You're sure, now."

"Henry, there's lots of stuff here to eat. And we're
enjoying ourselves."

He gets off the phone and says to Charlene, who is

at the old piano tenderly picking out a Chopin waltz, "We're eating alone. Henry's going to visit with Merry."

She turns, her eyes all big and full of light. He feels an unexpected rush of joy. It almost catches him off balance. It's a feeling like coming upon something that was lost, he thinks, and then finding it all of a sudden, there, beautiful and shiny as ever, staring up at you. He says, "I'll race you to the top of that hill. The one above the cabin."

"Don't blink," she says, spinning around. "I'm fast."

The tops of the hills, above Henry's cottage, are unploughed prairie grasses and wildflowers and wonderful scented plants that Charlene identifies for him, bergamot and sage and juniper. Beyond the hills, the fringes of delicate aspen and gnarled oak, are grain fields and prairie ditches full of sighing grasses, white and yellow clover, purple alfalfa. This is my country, he is thinking, this is the province where I was born, and I didn't even know it was here—so pure and pretty.

He makes pasta for dinner. He is excited to be alone with Charlene. Anything could happen. He puts lots of tomatoes in the sauce, all simmered in olive oil and garlic with basil from Henry's garden. Charlene finds a candle in the emergency kit in the cupboard. They eat at the table and look shyly at each other. Charlene has two helpings.

Later, they sit on the deck in the warm, dazzling night. They put their deck chairs together and sit with their feet up on the railing and talk. He cracks some stupid joke, and Charlene, giggling, reaches over and takes his hand.

They hold hands for a long time, neither of them saying a word. He marvels at this. At how electric her skin feels. At how tender and raw and wild and extreme he feels at the center of his heart. Around midnight, still holding hands, they fall asleep. He dreams that he is holding her heart. He dives with it to the bottom of the ocean and then rises with it and it is no longer a heart, it's Charlene. Her long hair twines around him. Her long, lush limbs twine around him. They are surrounded by warm water, and everything is pulsating.

At around three in the morning he wakes up, still holding her hand. He lifts it and kisses it. She starts, mumbles something. He leads her into the cabin and leaves her at her bedroom door. Henry's come back. His door is closed. Laker can hear him in there—his own particular way of almost whistling when he snores.

By seven o'clock Henry's in the shower. Then by seven-thirty he's out the door again. He leaves a note beside a plate of cinnamon buns and a big bowl of dark purple berries:

Beautiful day. Gone up the lake with Merry. She made the buns and the Creator made the berries. She wanted you to have some. We'll be back around noon. Please come and join us. Merry wants to give you "a feast." Until then, enjoy yourselves.

Love,
Grampa/Henry

"I don't know what to think," says Charlene, coming softly up behind him, resting her chin on his shoulder. "I'm supposed to be keeping an eye on Grampa. If Mom calls I don't know what I'll tell her. What do you think we should tell her?"

"We'll lie," says Laker, looking at the berries. He remembers a yellow pail. A bush pulled right down to bright green grass. A plump brown hand. A cascade of purple jewels. A voice singing softly. The image covers his vision, glowing like light, until it is all that he can see.

7 Charlene comes shining out of Heron Lake. Laker watches the way the water glides and falls in snaky rivulets down her body. He rolls onto his stomach. Then, when she's back, bent over and toweling her long, lemony hair, he gets up and runs until he hits the cold water. He swims out so far that a big sailboat glides between him and the shoreline. He dives, slides down until his lungs almost burst, and then torpedoes back to the surface, breaking through to the sunny air, the blue cloudless sky, the sweet-scented Manitoba heat.

He swims back slowly, then wades to shore, shakes out a towel, and lies down under the late-morning sun, beside Charlene. She turns her head. There is a little line of sand just under her bottom lip and down along her jawbone. She opens her eyes in the lazy heat, and he closes his. He can feel her watching him, and his heart pumps a little faster.

"Should we go back up?" she asks.

He opens his eyes. She has turned onto her side, her hipbone framed by a line of beach and sky. She rests on her elbow.

"Do you want to?"

"I don't know. What do you want?" Charlene's eyes are pools of greenish brown light.

He reaches up and strokes the sand from her chin, her lip, and his thumb stays on her lip. He watches carefully as she comes closer, leans over him, her hair grazing his shoulder. He shivers. She stops. "Are you cold?"

"No."

She moves closer, drops her head. Her mouth moves on his, softly, so softly. He sighs, pulls her gently all against him. Half of him can't believe this miracle is happening. The other half is diving headlong into the sweet wild center of her.

He is aware of nothing but Charlene until the dog hits them with a spray of water mixed with shale and

sand. They break apart, gasping, clutching towels,
wiping grit off their legs and arms. Tansi, shaking his
wild, wet fur several more times, is overjoyed to see
them. He dances around and bows, front legs extended, inviting them to play. Several lots down the
shoreline, just before a bar of land that juts into the
water, Henry and Merry are docking her boat.

Charlene looks at Laker, quickly kisses him again,
jumps to her feet, and holds out her hand. They
hold hands, until they are almost up to the boat—
Tansi in front, cavorting through the water, taking
bites from the little waves—and then Laker lets go.
He feels too weird about being so obvious in front of
Henry.

Henry, having difficulty getting out of the boat,
says to Merry, "Yesterday was a good day," and hur-
ries to add, "Didn't have a lick of trouble. I'll just sit
here for another minute."

"Take your time," Merry says. "It's a beautiful day,
my friend." She smiles as Laker and Charlene come
toward them, as she stands there waiting for Henry.
"There you are, Charlene," she says. "I haven't seen
you since you were fifteen. You grew up."

"That I did," says Charlene, smiling back.

"Come help your grandfather," says Merry. "He
could use your strong young arm today."

"Too late," says Henry clambering onto the dock.

He sways unsteadily, and Merry quickly gives him her arm. He looks very thin beside her. In fact, Laker thinks that maybe he's lost a bit of weight again. But then it's summer and he's been getting more exercise, which is very good for him. He'll probably live to be a hundred.

Henry finally catches his breath and says, "This is the young fellow who's staying with me."

"Yes. Laker," she says, carefully tilting her head, squinting at him against the sun's glare. "Come on up to my place. Are you hungry?"

"What have you got to eat?" Laker teases. Merry makes him feel giddy, just like a little kid.

"Ahhh!" she says laughing, patting his back. "You never told me, Henry, you had such a sunny boy staying with you."

"You didn't ask," Henry says with a chuckle.

8 "I rented a tiny cabin here, farther down the beach, for a few summers," says Merry. "After that I decided I'd like to live at Heron Lake all year round. So about ten years ago, around when I met Henry and Marianne, my son bought this bigger place for me and had it all fixed up. He's one of those bigwig writers in Toronto, so he can afford it." She says all this in a teasing way, and adds, "He's a good boy—when he isn't in trouble with women." She walks over to the fireplace, pulls back the screen, pokes at the dead coals.

Merry's place is grander than Henry's; the living room and kitchen all one big room, with a huge stone fireplace and an enormous view of the lake. Her deck has plants and little piles of white rocks and clumps of bone-white driftwood with knotholes that look like strange staring eyes or open mouths. He and Charlene go out there and look at the golden lake, the dark hills beyond, the lavender clouds drifting like dreams across the prairie sky.

Charlene nuzzles up beside him, whispers, "Hi."

"Hi," he whispers back.

She slips her hand in his. He bends and kisses her, tongue, lips, teeth. Looks into the cabin to see if Henry and Merry are watching, and they aren't, so he kisses her again. A faintly smoky scent rises in the wind from the beach, filling him with sudden disquiet. A memory begins to take form. He can feel its rumbling, heart-killing, joyless edges.

Charlene pulls away, her wide-open eyes on his eyes, his chin, his mouth, as if she is trying to trace him inside her own memory. As if she is somehow trying to memorize this moment. All this makes him sad. He doesn't know why. Placing her cool hand on his arm, she says, "I guess we've been out here long enough. We should go back in now."

They walk back inside, separating, not looking at each other. Henry has a fish on the counter, on some newspaper. It's about a foot long, its scales all gray and silvery, its mouth gaping, its eyes open, still bright.

"Merry and I caught three of these this morning," Henry tells Laker. "Well, in actual fact, she did. It was like watching a beautiful dance." He takes out a knife, runs it with some effort up the belly of the fish.

"Ahhhh!" says Merry, laughing. "Henry, you make me sound like a girl!"

The cut hand moves toward me. And then I can clearly see that it is not the old lady's. It's Audrey's. Her bloody hand, her bloody leg, her body, all cut.

The smell of the fish makes him feel sick.

Merry laughs again. "You're mesmerized. Come over here and talk to me." She's making a salad. She lays tomatoes on top with feathery green dill weed and bright orange flowers. "Nasturtiums," she says.

"What?" He is barely focusing. The smell of fish is so strong.

"The flowers," says Merry. "You can eat them. They're sweet and hot at the same time. You be careful," she says, looking back at the salad. "Young girls' hearts break real easy."

200   *She is crying. Kind of whimpering. Then she stops. She stops moving.*

Merry smiles, picks up a section of tomato, eats it. "You know, Charlene is so much like her grandmother. Today when I saw her it was like watching Marianne's ghost walk toward me. A blond ghost. But you don't have to look the same as somebody to have them be part of you. It's like they are always there, standing outside your flesh," she says, putting down her knife. "I've known Charlene since she was so high. That's a long time to know somebody. See their little ways. See them come along."

The old woman comes to her. Her hands flutter all over Audrey's face. She is calling to her. Saying her name over and over and over. Audrey isn't answering. Her face is as white as a stone.

"My mother's last name used to be Fontaine," Laker says all at once. "Audrey Fontaine."

She pulls a stool up to the counter, sits heavily. Lays her hand on his wrist, holding him in a trembling way. "Laker," she says. "My Laker boy." She shakes her head. "I was afraid to ask." She fumbles a tissue out of her sleeve, shakes her head again. Now she is openly weeping.

Henry, looking alarmed, comes to her, lays an arm around her. "What's wrong, Merry?"

Charlene gets up, too, from a chair where she's been flipping through a magazine. "What happened?"

A wave of heat spreads up Laker's body. He begins to shake. "Do you remember," he says, not taking his eyes off Merry, "when I was a baby and I stayed with you?" His breath comes too fast. He knows she is going to tell him something. Something that will change his life forever.

9 "You were with me for eight months. Your mom was here, too, with us for the first two of those months. Then you and I were alone together. You were so small. You turned two when you were still with me. I don't know how you could remember me, being so young as you were."

"She told me I made you up."

"Oh, I'm real. So are you. I can't believe I'm looking into your face. When Audrey came back for you she wouldn't tell me where she was going. I never once heard from her. I thought I'd never see you

again." She releases his hand, looks over at Henry.
"This is a miracle."

"Who was my father?"

Her deep eyes fly back and search his. He remembers her. She simply looks like an older old woman now. More wrinkles. Or maybe it's just that she's here in front of him and not back somewhere in a fog of time.

"He was a friend of my son, Gerald. Winston Dawes. He lived with us for a while."

"Winston Dawes?"

"Winston Dawes. That was your father's name. Is, I suppose. Nobody's heard from him in quite a while. He could be back in jail. In fact, that's a good possibility."

She reaches over and strokes his cheek. He feels weak and ill. He doesn't know if he really wants her to go on. He has a pretty good idea of what comes next.

"This is not a good story I'm going to tell you," she says gently. "Winston watched his mother die. Shot by his own father's hand. It was a hard, hard time for him."

"My grandfather murdered my grandmother?"

"That's right. Yes. I'm sorry."

He feels Henry's hand on his arm. Then he realizes Henry is in actual fact trying to hold him up, guide him, show him a stool that's been right in front of him the whole time. He sits, with Henry still standing beside him.

"Winston grew up real angry," Merry continues. "And then he met your mother, Audrey. I thought for a while they might just make it together. She was a happy little bird when she was with Winston. And Winston stopped doing all the bad things he'd been doing and worked two jobs after you were born. They were even talking about getting married. Then things started to happen. Winston lost one of his jobs. Couldn't find another. I noticed little things whenever they came over to visit. He'd pick a fight with her. She'd be in tears. He'd always be picking on her about this and that. Finally she left him. She asked if she could stay with me for a while. Until she got set up in her own place. Well, I liked your mom. She was like a daughter to me, and she needed mothering. Anyway, my husband, Clarence, had just died a few months before and I was missing him terribly—glad to have some company. Those first two months Winston never bothered her. Never touched her. He knew where she was, you see."

Merry looks at her hands. She's caught, it seems, in the memory of what she saw back then. When he was two years old. She is there. And now he can see it, too. A piercing hum has begun to grow inside his head.

"He would park across the street from my little home in Winnipeg and keep an eye on her," she continued. "Every second day or so, there Winston would be, just sitting in his truck. One day when he was not there I left Audrey and you alone. I went to the store. I wasn't away longer than a half an hour. But walking back with the groceries, I all of a sudden got a very bad feeling." She falls silent.

"He came into the house. They were yelling," Laker says softly, "and he . . . Something went wrong. . . ."

He remembers the noise. Covering his ears. And it is coming from me, he's thinking. But it's them, too. Too much noise in the room. I'm sitting on the floor. They're up above me, struggling. I'm seeing it, the blood. It's just red to me. I don't know what it is. I'm this little kid who doesn't know anything. But then when everything goes quiet, when everything stops and I look at my teddy bear . . . and the floor—she's there. She's lying there. And she's making this sound again. Something stops cold inside me. I see her mouth move, but I don't hear her anymore. I'm not even there, somehow. It isn't me watching her. I'm gone. My eyes, only, take it in. The face. The blood. The old lady moving toward her, saying her name over and over again. Saying "Audrey" with her soundless mouth.

IO

He walks with Henry down to the water. Merry and Charlene stay behind. Somebody has set an old yellow plastic lawn chair in the sand.

"Sit, son," Henry says.

"No, Henry, it's okay."

Henry sits but reaches up and touches Laker's arm and says again, "Sit. The sand's warm."

So he sits in the sand beside Henry's leg and, as Henry's hand finds its way to his shoulder, resting there, he stares out at the water, wiping his eyes with the back of his hand. They sit quietly for several minutes. He continues to wipe his eyes. Like a little kid he leans his head against Henry's knee.

"Well, son," says Henry. "It's been a helluva day."

He picks up a handful of sand, letting it sift through his fingers. A little black beetle, hiding under the sand or maybe burrowing there, scurries away. The way the sun hits it now, other colors are revealed, iridescent greens and blues. It isn't the way it first appeared, just a little black beetle. At first it seems confused about where it's going. But now it moves along the beach, parallel to the powerful waves, keeping a distance so it won't be washed away. He watches the beetle until it's just a speck moving along, a speck in the sunlight.

"I got a letter from her. From Audrey," Laker says. "She's asking if I'd like to come back. To maybe try living with them again."

Henry is quiet behind him. He isn't saying a word. Laker doesn't turn around.

"Well, son," Henry says at last, "I'm not going to be around forever."

"Don't say that," says Laker. "I really don't want to hear about it."

"But it's true. You and I both know it is. No use

fooling ourselves. We need to clear things up. I have to say that I just wanted this to be a good time for us all. And by and large, don't you think it has been?"

"What are you trying to tell me?"

"If you were to stick around," Henry goes on, "as I get more and more decrepit . . . Well, it might prove to be a real pain in the ass. You have to make your own decision about this, of course, and whatever it is, I'll honor it. But you know the truth, don't you? I'm kind of fading away here. That's just the way of it."

He thinks about Vera Lynne, her sudden change of heart, her tear-streaked face. While he was getting the mail and Audrey's letter, Henry was inside, telling Vera Lynne. That's why she let Charlene come along, why she told them *all* to have a good time. She really meant it. She truly wished them all well.

II Winnipeg is only a couple hours drive north of Heron Lake. When he called Audrey, he told her that he was in Manitoba, staying with Henry's family at the lake. He didn't specify which one—there are evidently hundreds of lakes in Manitoba. He just told her he'd drive into the city in the morning, be there by noon.

Henry says, "You've got your map."

"Yes."

"And the address?"

"Yes."

"You'll call if you have any trouble."

"Yes, Henry. I'll call."

"Well, then, you'd better go."

"Henry . . ."

"Yes, son."

"I just . . . well . . ." He can't say all that he wants to say. He can't bear to leave him.

"I'll see you in a few days, then," says Henry. "Don't you worry about me."

Laker enfolds him in a hug, feels the old man's bones against his chest. Is this what he came to Henry's to learn? That just as soon as you let yourself love someone, you have to lose them?

"Go now," says Henry, patting his back. "Go on, my boy."

He takes in the Manitoba landscape, this place of his birth: the fields of grain, the brilliant azure sky, the soft clouds as big as mountains. He rolls down the window, and his shirt flaps in the prairie wind.

Audrey and Rick's house, on a breezy bay with big overhanging trees, backs onto a large park. You can see the park from the street. He gets out of Henry's car and walks up the little sidewalk. Audrey has planted some yellow flowers against the house, and

they have recently been watered. He rings the door-
bell and waits. The house looks small, only big
enough for a couple with a baby, but then you never
know.

The door opens. Audrey steps out into the light,
holding Jem, a big baby with thick legs and blue eyes,
on one hip. She pushes back her hair, and her eyes
crinkle and narrow in the bright sunlight.

There is a long, painful break in his breath in
which he can see that she doesn't know whether or
not to touch him. So, instead, he hugs her, pulling
her small, birdlike body against him, and she makes
a little sound that is half laugh, half gasp. The baby
struggles, and they come apart.

"This is your brother," says Audrey, and she's wiping away big tears with her free hand, but more keep
coming.

Laker takes Jem's hand, the ends of the fingers,
giving it a little shake. "Hello, there," he says. He
avoids looking at Audrey. He doesn't want to cry.

Jem yanks his hand away, grasps Audrey's collar,
hiding his face in her neck. He has beefy little hands
that will probably one day hold a football and make
Rick feel all manly and pleased as hell. Even so,
Laker keeps staring at him. He can't take his eyes off
this baby he's seen only in photographs.

Jem shyly turns his face toward him again,

stretches out one arm, and head still resting against Audrey's chest, wiggles his fingers at Laker. He has a runny nose and the kind of loud breathing you think of with kids who have allergies. Petey used to have allergies. Gretel was always giving him medicine.

"Rick is out walking the dog," says Audrey. "He's home for a few days."

Jem hides his face again, then slowly lifts his head and lays an apple red cheek on Audrey's collarbone. He stares, eyes incredibly luminous, at Laker.

"Maybe he wants to see his big brother," says Audrey, pushing the baby toward him.

He doesn't want to hold him. Not yet. He's not ready for this. But suddenly the baby is in his arms, squirming around, looking back at Audrey, then, solemnly, at him.

"No," says Laker, firmly, handing the baby back to her. "He wants *you,* Audrey."

They go inside, sit in the gloom of Audrey and Rick's living room. Same living room, different house. But now there's Jem and a playpen and the smell of baby powder. The windows are all open and he can hear a wind chime in the back yard, and a breeze from the park is blowing right through the house.

"I'm going back to school in the fall," Audrey says nervously, and she sets Jem on the floor. He crawls

away, chubby hands and feet slapping against the
gleaming hardwood.

He thinks about the bear with the Santa hat, still back in Bemidji. If he stays in Canada, it'll be among the things that he'll ask Charlene to gather up and ship to him.

"So where is this lake you're at?" says Audrey, making conversation.

"It's called Heron Lake," he says, watching her carefully. "That's where Henry's cabin is. I didn't tell you that over the phone. I thought maybe you might like to explain things to me in person."

She puts her hands between her knees and leans forward, waiting, watching Jem. She's thinking. Slowly putting it all together. She seems about to say something. Then she lifts one hand to her hair, swivels away, lowers her head. Hand on her face. She's crying again. Her shoulders are shaking. She turns quickly to face him. "Is she still there? Does she still go out there in the summer?"

"She lives there now. I met her yesterday. Funny how things work out. She's an old friend of Henry's."

"I left you with her because I didn't know what else to do. You were just a baby. A year and a half. Not much older than Jem. Your dad was so big, Laker. I was scared of what he'd do if he came after us again.

That's why I left. That's why I didn't tell anybody where I was going."

"Mom, why didn't you tell me he almost killed you?"

"I just couldn't." She pauses, looks stricken, adds uncertainly, "I knew Merry would take care of you . . . until I could."

Jem comes crawling back across the floor; he's laughing and gurgling. He reaches Audrey's leg, grasps hold, pulls himself up. "He'll be walking soon," she says, stroking his head, looking sadly at Laker. "I'm sorry," she says, barely above a whisper, "for all that I've done. Maybe more for what I didn't do."

He thinks about the day he left. How violent he was. And how frightened she must have been. "No, Mom," he says, at last, leaning over, taking her small hand in his, "I'm sorry. I wish I'd known how bad he was to you. I wish that you had told me."

"Would it have made any difference?"

Rick comes through the back door just then, his familiar steps on the floor. And now when Laker remembers it in a flash of memory—heavy for such a small man. The dog comes rollicking into the room, big, brown, woolly, friendly looking. An unusual choice of dog for Rick. He'd have thought a meaner-looking dog, a protective-looking dog. It parks itself

at Laker's feet and, tongue wagging, looks back at
Rick, who lets out an actual chuckle. Then Rick
smooths back his hair, sits in a chair opposite Laker,
sits at the edge of it. He has a tan. It's improved his
appearance some. The dog goes over to him, and he
strokes it, looks at Audrey, then at Laker, then at
Jem, who laughs and leaves Audrey's leg and crawls
over to him. Rick picks Jem up and puts him on his
knee, rearranging, with a kind of clumsy tenderness,
his little shirt, which is white and embroidered with a
pale blue baseball.

"Laker's come for a visit," Audrey says to Rick.

"Oh," he says, and looks uncomfortable.

"I'm not staying," says Laker. He pauses, marveling
that he could actually say this out loud—even
though part of him wishes he hadn't—the part that
is still Audrey's little boy.

Audrey says, "But you've come all this way. . . ." her
voice trails off.

He looks at Rick, says awkwardly, "Sorry about that
time. About the fight."

"Oh, well," says Rick, with a funny little smile that
just misses making him kind of appealing.

At the door Audrey says again, "You're sure you
don't want to stay? You got my letter . . . letters?"

"Yes, Mom. I got them."

"Will I see you again?"

"Absolutely," he says, his voice catching in his throat. There's nothing left to do, or say. Yet there must be something. He then remembers the little fringed red leather pouch in his pocket, the whistle with the great piercing sound that he gave to Petey so long ago. That Petey gave back to him. He pulls it out and hands it to her.

"What's this?"

"It's for my little brother. He's going to love it." He hugs her again, and this time she hugs him back and holds on. "Maybe I'll come to Winnipeg for Thanksgiving," he says finally, breaking away from her embrace.

He goes out to Henry's car. He can feel her eyes on his back the whole time. He doesn't turn to wave. He gets in and drives away. Near the outskirts of the city he finds a pay phone.

The sun glances gold across the millions of trees that the city fathers had the foresight to plant. He makes his call. On the second ring Henry answers. Laker draws a long breath and then lets it out again, like a prayer.